CONSEQUENCES OF UNWISE CHOICES

MELANIE TAYLOR

AGD PUBLISHING SERVICES
UPPER MARLBORO, MARYLAND

AGD Publishing Services
Copyright © 2022 By Allison Gregory Daniels
All rights reserved.

Unless otherwise indicated, scripture quotations are from The Holy Bible, New King James Version. All rights reserved.

Printed in the United States of America

PAPERBACK ISBN: 978-1-7372867-6-9

EBOOK ISBN: 978-1-7372867-7-6

For details, Email: allisongdaniels@verizon.net

Contents

INTRODUCTION

It is hoped that this book will inspire and assist the reader in making wise choices and good decisions in life.

Yes, we are born into relationships with our parents, however, as we grow up and mature, we then move into additional relationships with relatives, and friends, as well as the dating scene, marriage, church, school, the workplace, and a host of other myriad environments, and beyond. Therefore, it is important to choose good sound relationships. In situations and matters of the heart, it is important to note that if we are offended, we must choose to forgive. First and foremost, it is important, no, it is undeniably necessary, to have a relationship with Jesus Christ as your personal Savior and Lord of your life. You see, the Holy Spirit put it on my heart to write this book over thirty years ago. The confirmation came when I seized the opportunity funded by my job to take an English and Writing course at a Community College. The professor enjoyed my essays; she would ask me to share my papers with the class. Although when my papers were returned to me, they had red marks all over them for grammatical errors; nonetheless, they would always be marked an A for the content. My professor commented on how interesting my essays were and she also told me that I would make a great writer one day. I was writing essays based on real-life experiences at the time. I wrote about a previous relationship with a drug dealer, and she found it fascinating. In that writing course, I realized I had a gift for storytelling.

The title for this book was given by the inspiration of the Holy Spirit. When I was thinking of writing this book, I kept hearing "Consequences of Unwise Choices".

This book herein shares my relationship stories, called "situationships" which is a trendy word now used to describe situations in relationships we find ourselves in. I found myself in "situationships" that could have destroyed my entire life. However, by the grace, mercy, and love of God, who protected and covered me during the unwise choices I made, I am who I am today, a virtuous woman of God. When I truly, intentionally, purposefully, and freely received Jesus as my Lord and Savior — I mean really saved, based on receiving God's amazing grace and love rather than receiving God under the law outlined in the Old Testament, God forgave me! God forgave my sins! And if God can forgive me of my sins, surely, I can and I choose to forgive others. As well as Jesus' redemptive power, instead of guilt and shame, redemption provided me with wisdom, peace, power, and lessons learned on my life journey. In Jesus, we are redeemed.

Colossians 1:14 "...in whom we have redemption through His blood, the forgiveness of sins."

Redemption is powerful. Now I look at my situationships as "life lessons learned". I take ownership of the unwise choices I made, and the consequences of heartaches, losses, painful and embarrassing experiences which revealed to me that I did not know who I was in Christ. Christ is the way to truth, and in Him is life and freedom; therefore, I have no shame in being completely transparent in sharing this story. The COVID19 pandemic was a great opportunity to write when the world's system was shut down, and we were socially isolated; making this the perfect time to write an inspirational new age story, with lots of drama, using fictional characters over real people, to inspire readers to make wise choices in life; to choose spirituality, to learn from mistakes, to always forgive yourself and others.

ACKNOWLEDGEMENTS

First, giving glory and honor to God, my Heavenly Father, who is the head of my life and who loves me, unconditionally. Dear God, because of Your great grace and love, today, I am the best version of myself because of You! AMEN

To my beloved husband David: You have supported me in all my endeavors. Thank you for accepting and loving me for my authentic self, for backing me in this quest, and for our unfailing love through it all. I love you, babe!

To my Parents: My late Father, John, was a great storyteller. I did not realize until this project, *that you were* pouring into me. I thank you daddy for being such an awesome earthly father. My Mother, Demetria, my greatest inspiration of faith, strength, hard work, and family. Thank you for teaching me to love all people –not just in words but in deeds. I love you both!

To my three beautiful, and amazing children: James, Britney, Ray, and your spouses. Thank you all for encouraging me to live my best life, to love completely, and laugh out loud. You and your families are my heartbeats.

To my loving grandchildren: Thank you for filling my heart with love and joy; may my legacy in this book be remembered as you make wise choices in life.

To my dear sister Michelle: Your memories are my memories, your stories are my stories. Thank you for sharing your enlightening views, and interpretations of life. To my BFF-sister Angie: Thank you for always having my back.

To my sister-girlfriend Marquita: Thank you for encouraging me during this process of writing, especially for all the late-night calls, for listening to my narratives, and for sharing your thoughts on this journey with me. Thank you for being unapologetically you and for always keeping it real.

To my mentor: Reverend Debbie Jefferson: Thank you for your example of a virtuous woman, your attentive ear, your spiritual guidance, and your prayers.

To my publisher: Reverend Allison Daniels: You have been an inspiring acquaintance, an incredible teacher in the writing course, and a woman of godly means and principles. Thank you and everyone in your publishing company who participated in this project. I appreciate you all.

Last, but certainly not least, to countless others who have inspired me and who are significant in my life; there are too many to name individually. I truly thank everyone who has supported and poured into me throughout my lifetime.

May God continue to richly bless each, and every one of you.

Agape, always.

FOREWORD

Minister Taylor's book is a page-turner! You will learn about managing adversity after adversity. She walks you through every intricate detail of her life from her childhood to her adulthood. She teaches, "You have to go through it to get to it" and, she has accomplished that through her faith and her belief.

She will have you smiling, crying, getting angry, and wanting to hug her as she walks you through her experiences of dealing with and overcoming betrayal, infidelity and lies. She reminds us of our duty as godly wives, to remain prayerful and steadfast –no matter how tough it gets. Minister Taylor will also encourage therapy during challenging times and reminds you to keep your pastor and spiritual-minded people in the loop to counsel you. However, with God as your helper, you will learn to forgive; you'll never go wrong with God because He will be there through your trials and tribulations –to see you through them all.

She ministers to us on bullying, entertaining bad

company, making unwise choices in relationships, domestic violence, all the while taking full responsibility for her own actions. Minister Taylor reminds us that it is wrong for either party to strike at one another because abuse is demoralizing.

What I love most about this book is that she keeps you engaged and inspired with scripture after scripture, The Word of God, to help encourage both married couples and single people, alike. She also reminds you that as "God blesses us, yes, the devil starts messing with us" but nevertheless, you be encouraged to persevere through it all.

You won't go wrong, and you won't waste your time reading this book. It will save marriages, help you to forgive others, and bring families closer together.

Tonya Barbee, MBA

Founder, I am Still a Rose, LLC

Best Selling Author, Coach, Inspirational Speaker

CHAPTER 1

Humble Beginnings

Many say that it does not matter where you start, but rather where you end up. I beg to differ. It does matter where you start from to where you finish.

Jeremiah 29:11 says, *"For I know the thoughts that I think toward you, says the Lord, thoughts of peace and not of evil, to give you a future and a hope."*

God has good plans for each of His children when we are born into this world. Therefore, it does matter where you start, but specifically, where you finish! When people understand your humble beginnings, they can understand how you came to be the person you are today. Our very first relationship starts at birth, with our parents. The Greek word *storge*: Means family love; it refers to natural or instinctual affection, such as the love of a parent towards their offspring and vice versa. So, this love is expressed as family love. And we had lots of love growing up in our entire family. I am a proud baby-boomer, where life was totally different from today's times, where there was absolutely no technology, other than a telephone and black and white television.

My parents were from a small town in Virginia. We came from humble beginnings, so when I was born, we did not have indoor plumbing in the house; the water came from a well outside of the house. We did not have the comforts of heaters or air conditioning units, but rather we had wood stoves and fireplaces during the winters and fans during the summers. We survived that simple lifestyle with love, faith, togetherness, good home cooking, and a village in raising children.

My maternal grandfather was a Reverend at the local church, which was right next door to the family home, about 300 feet away. The home was a small white bungalow, but we all seemed to fit in that small house, and we had large family gatherings. My mom had eleven siblings. Grandfather was a tall man; he reminded me of Dr. Martin Luther King when I was a little girl. Because he was all about unity and community, and he had a big heart. Both he and my grandmother were known in the community as hospitable to everyone who knocked on their door. Grandmother was one of the strongest women I had ever known. Although she was loving, she was strict at the same time. Grandmother was "gangster" and she had no problems checking you if you needed to be corrected. Grandmother also served in ministry alongside her husband. All the women in our family were strong women, and I do believe this was the result of grandmother's strength which was passed down through our generations. There was no need for our family members to have a lot of friends because we had each other. We enjoyed each other's company, we are music lovers, and we would get together to sing and dance, just having good times. I loved spending the summer in Virginia with my grandparents, aunts, uncles, and cousins. Our grandparents were the pillars of Christianity, that is laying the foundation of spirituality in our family's lives. My mother and her siblings grew up in church; some of them sang in the church choir and sang gospel music on the radio station. When you live in a small town, everyone knows everyone, and you get "gossip and tales." Having a reverend in your family, we could not get away with much. Even as a young grandchild, I felt as if we were always under the microscope with people in the community; in fact, it seemed like they were watching every little step we took, and this was hard, so I understood what it was like being a Preacher's Kid (PK) or grandkid. I remember several times my siblings, cousins and I were walking down the road to the general store; we would collect soda bottles from the side of the road and take them to the general store to exchange them for money to buy candy and snacks, and sometimes we would be so loud or just playing around, being kids and by the time we returned to the house, someone had called grandmother to let her know what we were doing. I remember one time my brother and cousin shook their finger at our grandparent's next-door neighbor, and she called our grandparents on them, and they both got a spanking. That was just how it was growing up in a small town; no questions asked. If an adult said you did something wrong, your parents, or grandparents believed them, and you would get a lecture or spanking. So, I was taught the word "respect" at a very young age. Respect became vital in my life with relationships – in fact, it came naturally, so when it was broken, it affected my wellbeing and trust.

Another vital part of my life was religion. When we visited with our grandparents during the summers, we had to attend church services, no matter how late we stayed up Saturday night. But I enjoyed Sunday school and church, especially the singing and dressing up in our Sunday's best. I remember looking at the Pastor, the deacons, and the reverends sitting in the pulpit and would think to myself that they must be very special people to God, and as a little girl, I never thought I would ever sit up there in the pulpit. So, when I became a minister and was invited to sit on the pulpit of my late grandfather, I was proud beyond measure.

Funny story: When I was a small child, there was a small office the Pastor, deacons, and reverends would come out of, and then onto the pulpit, but we were never allowed to go into that office, so when I finally was able to go in there, it was like finding a hidden treasure. When our grandparents cleaned the church, we would go with them, but again, we were never allowed to even step foot on the pulpit let alone go into that office. And now –now that I am all grown up, and eligible to go into that little office, it was nothing special about it at all, a little office with an old desk and chair.

My paternal grandfather was a carpenter and farmer, and he was well known for building and fixing houses in that community. I was told that he could fix anything – that he was a jack of all trades.

Both sets of grandparents were members of the same community church, and they all served in ministry in some compacity. My dad was the youngest of six siblings. When he was born, my grandfather was already fifty years old. My grandfather lived to be close to a hundred years old before he transitioned. My dad shared stories about them growing up; growing up with horses, the many livestock, the vegetable gardens, and they only needed a few staple items like flour, milk, and sugar, from the general store. My dad shared with us that my grandfather became very ill when he was a young boy and he had to drop out of school to take care of his father, help take care of the home and their property. Daddy told us that he was out in the fields one day, and he prayed to God for his father's healing, and yes, Praise God, his father survived his illness and lived a very long life afterwards. They moved from Virginia to Baltimore, MD when I was a baby. And whenever we visited them, my grandfather would cry when he saw my older brother; he loved my brother dearly. I do not remember much about my paternal grandmother other than she was a very short beautiful, sweet little lady and she loved cats. Before we moved to Washington DC, my parents lived in their house. My first traumatic experience was that of a cat jumping into my playpen, breathing over my face. When my father came into the room, the cat quickly jumped out. That cat seemed like a lion to me. And that experience caused me to be afraid of cats. People say, fear is taught, so yes, I agree, and fear comes from traumatic experiences which can shape us.

The Word says in 2 Timothy 1:7 *"For God has not given us a spirit of fear, but of power and of love and of a sound mind."*

Honestly, I am still working out that scripture when it comes to cats.

One time in Sunday school a teacher asked us what were we afraid of? I replied, cats and she said, *"well, you better be a good Christian girl because if you do not live a Christian life, you will go to hell and be put into a den with cats"*. She told me to receive Jesus as my Lord and Savior, and that He would protect me, just like Daniel in the lion's den. God protected Daniel when he got thrown into a lion's den for not worshiping King Nebuchadnezzar's idol gods. She explained to us that if we obey God's commandments and continue to serve God, ~~when~~ *until* *we die, we would be with God.* That Lion's Den story was so scary. I tell you, I was indeed traumatized. All I knew was that I did not want to go to hell, and she got me to receive Jesus as my Lord and Savior right then and there. Later, I got baptized, and I have been a Christian ever since.

My Christian foundation was surrounded by the good intentions of God-fearing people. They were doing their best to lead us to salvation. Growing up I feared God in a tormented or in a distressing way. I viewed God as being up there in Heaven as the strictest authority in the whole wide world, like a policeman with a big stick, ready to beat me down whenever I sinned or made an unwise choice. I feared God, but not in a reverential manner, but rather in a judgmental and consequence manner. But this is not the God I serve today. God is love and love is God. 1 John 4:8 says: *"He who does not love does not know God, for God is love."*

Although we did have plenty of religion and traditions, a personal relationship with God would take both many years and understanding the Word of God, to grow and mature in Him. Some of the traditions we had were that on New Year's Eve, a *man* (not a woman) must walk across the doorstep *first* when the year changed because this would be a sign of fortuity or favorable chances, occurrences. And, at midnight, we must be down on our knees in prayer when the new year came in if we were home and not at Watch Night service. Also, eating black-eyed peas and pork on New Year's Day for good luck and prosperity. Last but certainly not least, our parents would allow us to have a sip of champagne to toast in the New Year, which was exciting for a kid.

My folks were honest, hard-working people, and they were always pleased and grateful for our blessings. I do not have any excuses for making unwise choices like some other children have because of possibly, an absentee parent in the home, but at any rate, still, I made unwise choices of my own accord, which was due to me not knowing God's Word, and being disobedient. The costs and consequences were the result, and we rarely anticipate the consequences of our choices. I had to learn the hard way, but you do not have to learn the hard way; read this book and learn the right way. I am grateful because God was always with me. I am here today because of Him. God deserves all the glory, honor, and praise for my deliverance and transformation.

MY FIRST ENCOUNTER WITH GOD:

I was about eight or nine years old and on this one specific day, I went to the Catholic church with my neighbor, who would babysit us when all the adults went out. We would walk to the church. And when we walked into the church, I followed what she did; she dipped her finger into the holy water and placed it on her forehead and shoulders and made the sign of the cross. Then we went to our seats, we kneeled and sat, the congregation would chant some words, we would stand, then we would kneel and sat. Then the priest held up a beautiful gold chalice cup with the fruit of the vine in it. He would recite something, after which, the congregation would repeat it. I do not remember what it was, and then, the people all stood up, they made a bald fist and pressed it on the middle of their chest. So, I followed what they were doing, but when I placed my fist onto the middle of my chest, I felt a burning sensation in the place where my bald fist rested. Initially, it scared me, but I knew at that time God had touched me because I felt His presence. And I do believe God has been with me and covering me ever since that day.

When I say cover me, I mean, from physical death, diseases, imprisonment, drug addiction, and a life of crime. But you must understand that sin has consequences. My journey with unwise choices is about trusting people and being gullible. Those unwise choices taught me early in life many lessons, which helped to develop and mature me into the person I am today. You will see how I was able to forgive the people who hurt me, and how I have come to love them, unconditionally, because I now understand that the devil was trying to destroy me. The devil used many people to harm me, but God's grace covered me. What the devil meant to destroy, God turned each situation around for my good and for lessons to be learned.

John 10:10 says: *"The thief does not come except to steal, and to kill, and to destroy. I have come that they may have life and that they may have it more abundantly."*

This scripture will help you to understand that the devil is a thief, and his assignment is to steal your purpose, kill your dreams and destroy your life. Therefore, the wise choice is to choose Jesus and become His follower.

GROWING UP IN WASHINGTON, DC:

In the sixties, Washington, DC had many segregated sections in the city. When we moved to Washington, DC we moved to southeast, Anacostia. Our parents provided a clean, healthy environment for us children. They would clean the inside as well as the halls of our apartment building and people thought they were the resident managers of the building. But this was the type of hardworking people they were.

Once in Washington DC, we had all the conveniences of living in a city. Every Sunday morning, whether we attended church or not, we listened to gospel music and sermons on the radio. One Sunday morning, I remember breaking out into a dance-off on church music, and then immediately I was chastised. I was taught that you don't dance to gospel music, which was not accurate, according to the Word of God, because dancing is a form of worship. At the Tabernacle of David, David danced out of his garments worshiping the Lord; see 2 Samuel 6:14-22. However, back then, dancing to gospel music was forbidden in our family, as this was the legalistic way we were raised. I guess at that time they did not know that King David danced before the Lord passionately and that he danced right out of his garments. Also, we were not allowed to take Holy Communion unless we were baptized. They did not know that communion is the children's bread, and for the believer, taking Holy Communion was significant and this shows Jesus' death, burial, and resurrection –along with His healing power until He comes back for the church.

1 Corinthians 11:26 says: *"For as often as you eat this bread and drink this cup, you proclaim the Lord's death till He comes."*

This scripture says nothing about being baptized. Again, these were the traditions and religion of my upbringing.

Growing up, I have many fond memories as a little girl on Sunday nights, when both of my parents would watch that all-time favorite western television show, Bonanza. Those who remember it, the music was that of a horse-riding tune and my dad would be my horse and give me a ride on his knees and my mother would be my brother's horse and give him a ride on her knees. This was one of the most loving memories of being a little girl, and holidays were always a big deal. On Christmas, daddy would take us to downtown DC on "F" Street to the big department stores to see the Christmas decorations in Woodward & Lothrop, Garfinkel's, Hecht's, and to many others. There were also smaller store windows that were beautifully decorated as well. Daddy took us to the circus, the playgrounds, parades, the zoo, and every Saturday daddy would take us to McDonald's after a trip to the laundromat. In those days you could get a hamburger, French fries, and a coke for only one dollar. Life was simple and easy, so other than that cat traumatizing me, I would say, I had a normal, fine life, and a healthy childhood.

By the seventies, life started to change. My two aunties who lived with us got married and moved out of our home. And for the first time, it was only my siblings (an older brother, twins — a boy and a girl and me (I'm the middle child)) and our parents living together. Our parents worked two jobs each, so for the first time since our aunties moved out, once we were out of school, there was no adult supervision in the home. My older brother and I were in charge, and we did pretty much whatever we wanted at the ages of twelve and thirteen. We were children trying to be grownups, and that's when the unwise choices began.

1 Corinthians 13:11 *"When I was a child, I spoke as a child, I understood as a child, I thought as a child; but when I became a man (or woman), I put away childish things."*

So, when I was a child, I spoke, acted, and understood as a child, but when you are a child trying to be grown, you will make unwise choices. We got into some serious mischiefs. My brother had all the latest albums. We would have a good time playing music, dancing, and having our friends over, unsupervised, so you can only imagine how that went. We were faithful Soul Train watchers. My cousin C called me "Soul Train Girl", because I went to a party with her one night, and I was doing all the Soul Train dances; her friends laughed at me, because although we did not live in Los Angeles, CA (where Soul Train was taped), we had our own latest dance moves in the DMV (District, Maryland and Virginia), and it was so not the west coast vibes!

Looking back over my life, I believe that both parents working two jobs and being out of the home during the evenings affected my reasoning as a teenager. People would often say, "there is no handbook on parenting". I disagree with that; I believe the Bible is the handbook and road map to a successful life. The Bible covers any and every situation we deal with in life. Our parents did the best they could in raising us, they worked hard to make a better life for our family. But when you know better, you can do better; the Bible clearly states it is not wise to leave children unattended. Therefore, no excuses parents!

Proverbs 29:15, *"The rod and rebuke give wisdom, but a child left to himself brings shame to his parent."*

Lessons Learn: Children need adult supervision. Remembering the mischiefs and things we got into growing up, after I had my children, I never took a part-time job because I know, this can potentially cause the child to get into mischief, resulting in bringing shame to the parent as the scripture states. Also, think about when parents are away from their children, they may not be aware of what the child/children are experiencing, especially in school. My parents never knew that I was bullied in school. I just never spoke about it with my parents, but the experience affected me both positively and negatively.

THE BULLY:

I had been coping with "situationships" since elementary school. I had a bully who harassed me the entire school year until I faced my fears and stood up to him. I bet every generation has dealt with a bully (in school or in their community), and that is one thing that has not changed. I never told my parents about this boy physically abusing me. It was in third grade and this bully would kick me under the desk, and my knees would be bruised. After our school day ended, I would be the first to get in line to be dismissed, and when that bell rang, I would take off running, but that bully would catch up with me, and start pushing me in the back. I would constantly tell him to *stop pushing me*. He would laugh and continue until I turned on my street. I remember that school year I got sick with the mumps and was out of school for over a week. That was the best week of my little life to be away from him. By springtime, I had enough of him pushing me around. One day, while in class, I walked past him, and he stuck his foot out and tripped me up. I was so mad and tired of him messing with me, I turned around and windmilled that joker with both my hands balled into fists, punching him in the face and each time I hit him, he hit the back of his head on the wall. I can remember this incident like it was yesterday. The teacher had to separate us. During those days, teachers could spank you and they could hit you with their ruler; this teacher made us both stay after school. I was terrified of those thirty minutes of detention because I just knew he was going to beat me up on the way home. But to my surprise, we both walked together and from that day forward, he never bothered me again. This situation gave me confidence to fight for myself and face my fears to survive living in Washington DC. Also, one of my aunties did not play when it came down to bullying; she would be ready to make us fight any time and any place. And if she found out that I did not take up for myself, she would threaten to give me a whipping, so I was not about to get two whippings. For some reason, I managed to hide that bully from her. My auntie was "gangster" like my grandmother. She made us fight for ourselves because she was not always going to be around to protect us, and we had to survive living in SE Washington, DC.

Because of the bullying experience I encountered, I believe that when a guy would hurt me (in a relationship), this would provoke me to become physical by hitting the person and I would be all up in that person's face; people who think they know me would not believe this about me, but it's true. Being bullied was a traumatic experience; I believe the experience shaped me into becoming passive/aggressive throughout my life regarding being hurt or disrespected, until I got delivered.

Regrettably, I developed a negative behavior, which was a

result of that traumatized experience. Remember I talked about the word "respect". Therefore, when I felt disrespected in a relationship, I became abusive and uncontrollable because I viewed myself as being very loyal to the person in the relationship, so, when they betrayed me, my feelings were hurt and I became both angry and physical because I wanted them to feel my pain, which caused me to have anger management issues.

Although I have always had an outgoing personality, I've always been a people person, very sociable, with a constant smile and laughing out loud, and very talkative, however, if someone crossed me, I would become hostile and violent. But God! It was God who humbled and delivered me, by His grace and His mercy; God was so merciful to me, and I can come to Him boldly like I never had a sin issue in my life.

Hebrews 4:16 "*Let us, therefore, come boldly to the throne of grace, that we may obtain mercy and find grace to help in time of need.*" AMEN

Thank you, Jesus, for Your mercy and grace!

Now, from humble beginnings to boyfriend-girlfriend thang.

CHAPTER 2

"Therefore do not be unwise but understand what the will of the Lord is." Ephesians 5:17

My first real relationship started in seventh grade, at age thirteen. I can't even imagine my children being in a relationship at the age of thirteen. But this specific boy made me feel all bubbly and nervous on the inside; my stomach would be in knots when I was around him. What in the world did I know about love! I looked up the Greek word eros and it represented my feelings about Jay. Eros is passion, lust, pleasure. It's an appreciation for one's physical being or beauty and is driven by attraction and sexual longing. It describes desire and is most like what we think of as romantic, passionate love between marriage partners, at least in the earlier stages of courtship, when you can't get enough of each other, that is.

Eros is what I was feeling toward him because he made me feel different; feelings I never felt before when I was in his presence. I daydreamed that one day we were going to get married, live in a house with a white picket fence, just like the perfect family in the movies or storybooks. We would have three children and live happily ever after. He made me feel the way I felt when I first saw Michael Jackson on the Ed Sullivan show. I dreamed of marrying Michael Jackson which may have been every girl's dream at the time, and I still love MJ, but when I met Jay, reality kicked in; I understood that I could not move to *Indiana* and marry MJ, so Jay became the love of my life.

Jay was not like the other boys in the community. He acted older than a thirteen-year-old would generally act; perhaps it was due to him being very independent. He hung out with the older guys in the community, and it seemed as if he was pretty much living on his own, a lot. He was popular and known as a "bad boy". At the beginning of our relationship, we were two innocent kids, having fun with our peers, playing around, chasing each other, and as they say, "love taps, a kiss" just being silly kids. Jay had a lot of girlfriends following him around. As time went on, I discovered so much more about him. He had always been a womanizer all his life. When Jay started paying attention to me, although I knew he had other girlfriends, it did not diminish my desire to constantly be around him, and then become his special girl. We lived in the same townhouse developments and by the time I turned thirteen, I wasn't that chubby little girl anymore, and I then began to turn the heads of the boys in our community. At the beginning of school, we would get new clothes, and I would wear an afro or poof-balls, bell bottoms, vests, short shirts with colorful patterns, and hip hugger jeans. Yes, I was that girl! We always were well dressed in our new school clothes, and they were of the latest fashion: being well dressed is another important factor in my upbringing and shaped me into the person I am today. On Christmas, we would get new clothes. At the beginning of summer, new clothes, shorts, hot pants, and halter tops! Easter, outfits! In our community fashion mattered, the way you dressed mattered because it represented status and popularity. And maintaining that lifestyle costs money.

Jay's house was on the top of the hill of our complex and my house was located on the next level down. Jay later told me, that when we walked home together and he would arrive at his house first, he would run into the house before I would get to my house and watch me from his window. That was flattering to me because I felt a certain way about him; that sharing won my heart. Then we started calling ourselves boyfriend-girlfriend at that time which meant proclaiming we were exclusive. He promised that he would stop talking to the other girls. We would talk on the phone for hours. He walked me to classes, bought me snacks and little gifts like earrings and bracelets, which was a big deal at that age; he was extremely thoughtful, sweet, and kind toward me.

Jay had his freedom beginning at the age of thirteen which was quite early than 18-year-old young boys, but at any rate, Jay did not have a curfew. He smoked cigarettes, marijuana, and he would constantly hang out late at night and on weekends, going to parties. He seemed to always get into a lot of trouble and fights; later I discovered those beefs would be about someone's girlfriend he was messing around with. He was the type of guy you would not want your daughters to date or hang around with. Jay always seemed to have quite a bit of money on him, and I found out that he preferred to steal what he wanted, just to see if he could get away with it and keep his *own* money in his pocket. I recall one time, when we were fifteen or so, we cut school and went shopping downtown Washington DC, on "F" Street, to the big Macy's Store for Christmas. Jay had a pocket full of money. I had no money on me, not even enough money to get home on the bus. I was totally dependent upon him. Anyways, he wanted these Ralph Lauren polo socks, so instead of buying them, he stole the socks. An undercover cop watched Jay as he grabbed my shopping bag and tried to put the socks into my bag, but I pulled my bag away from him and I said, *no put it in your bag!* He did, then, we both decided to sit down in Macy's café to have lunch before we left. The undercover cop did not bother us until we proceeded to walk out the door. I was so glad that I told him to put those socks in his shopping bag, because when we were on our way out of the store, the undercover police officer grabbed him, threw him on the floor, and handcuffed him. When that police officer stopped Jay, my heart dropped to my stomach. He put those handcuffs on Jay so tight, Jay was shouting at the officer to, *please loosen the handcuffs, my wrists hurt; these handcuffs are on too tight!* The officers said you should have thought about that when you stole those socks. He took Jay to the back of the store to call his parents. But before they went to the back, the officer asked me if Jay was my brother? I said no, he is my boyfriend, sounding stupid. He said, I was watching you and I saw you pull your bag away when he tried to put the socks into your shopping bag. Then he said, *you need to leave him alone because he is going to get you into trouble if you keep hanging with him.* He said that is not the way a nice guy would treat you. That officer warned me to leave Jay alone. But I did not listen to sound advice. Once the officer took Jay to the back of the store, I was left alone to fend for myself, and as I stated, I did not have a dime to my name. I walked to the bus stop. I was so nervous and shaken from what had just happened, that I did not know what to do. There were no cell phones back then. Lucky for me, it was after school hours, and students were getting on the bus. I walked around like a panhandler asking people for money so I could get on the bus and go home. Finally, a student gave me a bus token and that was how I made it home. This was my first warning. But, nonetheless, I did not take heed to that warning from the police officer; a bad decision –another unwise choice.

Growing up in SE Washington, DC was rough, but it was home for us. Washington DC afforded great opportunities to be successful. I started my first government job at sixteen, working for the Federal government during the summers. I remember being asked one time where did I live, and when I replied that I lived in SE Washington, the employees would ask questions about the safety of my community. Was I afraid to live there? I would look confused, with my reply, "no, why would I be afraid"? Of course, they were non-African American employees and those comments made me feel degraded about my environment. People will judge you by where you live. Honestly, I just thought crime was a part of everyday living in the city. I had friends who committed crimes just to survive. There were number-runners, drug dealers, and thieves who boosted (stole) clothes and other merchandise to sell in the community. One time, this guy in our neighborhood told my dad that he was selling television sets for a cheap price so my daddy and brother drove him to an apartment building, gave him the money, and he never came out of that building, they waited for hours, my dad was so mad, and when someone told my dad they saw that man in the neighborhood (I believe it might have been Jay) daddy got his gun and was going after that man. I was so scared that if my daddy killed that man, he was going to jail. Thank God, my daddy did not find him.

Jay would be all over the neighborhood. He knew everything that was going on in the streets. I felt safe with him. When thieves in the community started breaking into people's houses, no one touched my family's home; they knew better so I felt safe in my community, as long as Jay was around.

Most of the residents in my community were hard-working people. Washington DC offered numerous opportunities for employment, and some very prominent people came from the southeast area. It was all about making wise choices with your life, and if you did, you could be very successful.

Jay was sweet and kind to me, but he could be a cold-hearted and vicious person if he needed to be because he had a dark and mischievous side. I personally saw him kicking and beating up this guy on the streets, and he had no mercy on the guy.

My daddy was okay with me dating Jay, but my mom was not fond of it. When my mom found out he was selling drugs, she really did not like or want me associating with him. Like any good mother, she was concerned that I would get caught up in drugs, get in trouble, or even killed by being associated with him. She warned me, just like the Macy's Department Store's undercover officer. But that did not stop me either. I just loved that guy! He was my guy, and I thought I could not live without him. Yet another unwise choice.

1 Corinthians 15:33 *"Be not deceived: evil communications corrupt good manners."*

Mothers know best! Now, at this point of our relationship, we were engaged in sexual immorality. I had an ungodly soul tied to Jay, due to being tied to him sexually. I believed we were going to get married, obtain employment, and have our own family. He was my first love, my first everything. He brought excitement and adventure into my little boring country and mundane life. I was attracted to the bad boy. My love for him reminded me of the show "For My Man" except, I was not willing to indulge or commit any crimes for my man. I was gullible about love, but not about my freedom. I heard horror stories about the things that happened in prison, and I wanted no parts of that. Going to prison was not an option for me. I wanted to be in Jay's life apart from his criminal activities. But how can you be with a bad boy, and not jeopardize your freedom or safety?

Looking back and reflecting on some of the situations he put me in, it is a miracle I never got arrested. And

36

that is the reason I am very grateful to God. I know God was always protecting me, ever since I was a little girl, having a supernatural experience when God touched my heart at that Catholic Church. God kept me safe from harm during my unwise choices, and He deserves all the glory, honor, and praise for keeping me during my darkest hours. God had good thoughts and plans for me.

Jeremiah 29:11 *"For I know the thoughts that I think toward you, saith the Lord, thoughts of peace, and not of evil, to give you an expected end."*

It was my Heavenly Father watching over me. God was preparing me for such a time as this, to share the good news of His love, and His watchful–faithful eye on me during these unwise choices I made.

Romans 5:8 *"But God demonstrates His own love toward us, in that while we were still sinners, Christ died for us."*

While I was being disobedient, God still demonstrated His love toward me. I was resentful as a teenager because I was made to be responsible and look out for my younger siblings which prevented me from hanging out with my friends. But I sure do appreciate it now, because having responsibilities kept me out of trouble. Some of my friends would tease me, calling me Hazel the maid. Hazel was a comedy television show about a live-in maid with her employers the Baxter Family back in the late sixties and early seventies. The peer pressure I received from my friends to hang out with them, but I couldn't because of family obligations, caused me to go through a season of being rebellious and disobedient to my parents, which was something that I am not proud of.

Lesson Learned: So here is the lesson. *Be a leader and not a follower.*

Just like with today's challenging teenage culture, also being a teenager back then was very challenging, to say the least, so trying to fit in with our peers and be a part of the popular elite group, as with most of the teenagers in my neighborhood were popular for doing the wrong things; they were not positive examples in the community. Being a follower can result in you making an unwise choice: know one thing for certain, I was not a follower when my friends were getting into trouble.

I remember a time when some girlfriends had stolen someone's credit card. They skipped school, took that card, and went shopping. They asked me if I wanted to go with them, but I said, "no thanks, y'all go on". They came back with new clothes. But sure enough, they got caught and arrested. You see, then, I was so focused on my relationship with Jay, being his girlfriend and all, but I was not about to commit crimes *with* him or *for* him, or anyone else, for that matter. I distinctly told him that "I would absolutely not have anything to do with committing crimes"! I would tell him no in a minute, with no hesitation whatsoever! One time Jay asked me to go pick up an overnight bag out of his car which was towed; he stated he could not get there, and he did not want it to be stolen and it was raining outside. So, I said, yes, I will pick it up for you. On my way to the towing lot, my car spun around in the middle of the street! Not hitting anything, at that point, I thought to myself, this must be a sign for me not to proceed to the towing lot. I followed my intuition, and I went home. He called a few hours later, asking if I picked up the bag and when I said, no he was very upset with me. I asked what was in the bag so important? He said a package that belongs to someone. I knew what that meant, and I was glad I followed what most would say, intuition. Now, looking back, that was the Holy Spirit directing my steps. Jay was trying to pull or usher me to come into his world at every twist and turn. But that lifestyle was not for me. So, when I heard about him and some random chick being together, he would say, stuff like, *"Well, you couldn't or wouldn't go with me"* or he would say, *"Well, you wouldn't or couldn't do it for me, so I had to get someone else!"* This was sort of his way in trying to manipulate me to be about that lifestyle or his lifestyle.

Now, let's return to *bad company corrupts good character.*

We would skip school and hang out at his house. Later,

I became pregnant at 17 and I had the baby at 18. As I stated earlier, I had an *ungodly* sexual soul tie to Jay. *A soul tie is like a linkage in the soul realm between two people. It links their souls together, which can bring forth both beneficial results, and negative results. The positive effect of a soul tie: In a godly marriage, God links the two together and the Bible tells us that they become one flesh.* And Jay had an ungodly sexual soul tie with me and yes, you guessed it, with many other young girls at the same time. An ungodly soul tie can happen when you desire love, approval, or affection from someone other than God. In other words, an ungodly sexual soul tie is when a person is sexually bonded to another person who is not their spouse, and you have an emotional attachment to them because of your mysteriously longing for that person. Now, you might ask yourself or think to yourself, "*And how do you know if you are in an unhealthy soul tie relationship?*" Well, it's when you will allow your sexual partner to cheat, abuse, and disrespect you, which I did many times, and they cause you to take your spiritual focus off God. But the Bible says:

1 **Corinthians** 6:18 *"Flee fornication. Every sin that a man doeth is without the body; but he that committeth fornication sinneth against his own body."*

The first time I caught Jay cheating on me we were talking on the phone, and I told him I was coming to his house to see him. He started making up excuses why I should not come, so I knew something was wrong. He had never told me not to come before, and because of the ongoing thoughts and knowledge I already had, I went to his house anyway. He looked out the window and he saw that it was me. He would not open the door, so I got mad, and I started knocking and kicking on his door, repeatedly –loudly. He still had not opened the door, so I returned to my house, got a knife, and went back to his house, trying to pick the lock on his door lock. I tore a hole in the screen door. Even writing this sounds crazy. In my mind and while this is happening, I have a flashback of my time in elementary school, fighting the bully who had hurt me. At this point, I am committing vandalism to their property. I thought I had the right to do what I was doing because of our boyfriend-girlfriend thang. However, I was acting like a big fool.

Proverbs 12:15 *"The way of a fool is right in his own eyes: but he that hearkeneth unto counsel is wise."*

Instead of seeking wise counsel and or communicating this with my parents, I hid this and covered up the foolishness going on in my life. If I knew then what I know now, I would not have made this unwise choice in having a relationship with Jay. How many times have you said that? If I would have sought wise counsel, I do believe my life would have gone in another direction had

I known better. Especially if I was more obedient to my parents.

Ephesians 6:1-2 *"Children, obey your parents in the Lord: for this is right. Honour thy father and mother; which is the first commandment with promise."*

Now, I am constantly sharing with our young people to please, obey your parents, honor them, because they truly do have your best interests at heart. If you do not listen to your parents, like me, you may face severe consequences pursuant to the unhealthy and unwise choices you make, which may affect you for the rest of your life. Yes, I thought I was grown. I was just doing my own thing. And when we do our own thing without God, we open the door for the devil, and we give him a license to occupy our thoughts and cause us to react in a negative and harmful manner, which can lead to a wide road to destruction.

Matthew 7:13-14 *"Enter ye in at the strait gate: for wide is the gate, and broad is the way, that leadeth to destruction, and many there be which go in thereat: Because strait is the gate, and narrow is the way, which leadeth unto life, and few there be that find it."*

I had dreams –big dreams and goals. I had talent. I had skills. I wanted to be a professional dancer on Broadway. I had participated in talent shows and school events and I had been taking dance classes since I was seven years old. I enjoyed the performing arts environment.

I remember participating in a talent show at my cousin's high school; he was the producer of the show. The whole family came out to support the event, including Jay. After the talent show was over and everyone was complimenting me on my performance, Jay got jealous and highly upset with me. It seemed as if he was constantly getting an attitude or jealous after these types of events, so I eventually stopped performing. I did not understand at the time that I was allowing him to manipulate and control my life. You see, I really thought he was showing me that he loved me, so I did not pursue my dreams of dancing because I loved Jay more than my dreams. Unfortunately, I allowed what he felt and how he felt to stop me from dancing and performing in the arts. I even auditioned to attend The Duke Ellington School of the Arts, in Georgetown. I made the first cut, but I never went back to the school. I decided not to pursue my dreams of dancing, partly because Jay did not like other men watching me dance.

In addition to how Jay felt, another reason I did not go back to Duke Ellington was because I would have had to leave home very early in the mornings to catch public transportation to Georgetown from SE Washington, and during that time, there was a report that a rapist was lurking in our community. I was afraid to be alone, which was a wise choice. I ended up going to the local High School and catching public transportation with a group of neighboring students.

So, during my junior high school years, I encountered a traumatic experience which totally affected my decision to not attend Duke Ellington, so it was not totally about Jay's discontent with my dancing. One day during my middle school years, a guy tried to sneak up on me, however, he did not have the opportunity to grab or take advantage of me. It was in the same neighborhood where another young girl was violated; the guy grabbed her from behind and took her behind our junior high school and assaulted her. On this same day, I was walking home alone during lunch period. Normally other students in the neighborhood would be walking home for lunch as well, but no one was around on this day. My older brother was home, fixing lunch and watching "The Young and the Restless" soap opera; he acted years beyond his age. My brother was driving at the age of 12 or 13. He was dating grown women while he was in high school – no joke! He was home that day, and he couldn't believe it when Jay and I told him what had just happened to me. When I was walking down the street alone, I saw Jay talking to one of the neighbors; he then told me that he was coming to my house, so I decided to hurry ahead of him, and in a playful manner, I hid beside a house. I was planning to jump out in front of him to startle him; however, when I was standing there, waiting, with my head turned towards the right, I felt someone walking towards me on the left side, and when I turned my head to look to my left, this man was tiptoeing toward me very slowly and creepy like. When I saw him, I ran from the side of the house, back up the steps towards the direction in which Jay was coming. When Jay saw me, I had a look of terror in my eyes, as if I saw a ghost –well I did! This guy looked creepy! Jay asked what was going on? I told him that this man was coming toward me, and I think he was going to grab me. Jay did not hesitate or think twice; he immediately ran down the stairs in the direction I came from and when that guy saw Jay, he took off running into the woods. Jay picked up some big rocks and started throwing them at the guy, telling him to stay away from the area. So, you see, yet another reason why I was totally lost in him and had my hooks into him because he was fearless. And because of that, I felt safe around him. I am not sure what would have happened to me if Jay was not there at the right time! He was my hero and I loved him even more after that incident. So, when we told my brother what had just happened, my brother said not to tell our parents because they would worry so we never spoke of the incident. This was truly God's protection over me, and He just happened to use Jay.

Psalms 91:3-4 *"Surely he shall deliver thee from the snare of the fowler, and from the noisome pestilence. He shall cover thee with his feathers, and under his wings shalt thou trust: his truth shall be thy shield and buckler."*

It was God who delivered me from the snare of that demonic man. God is my refuge and my strength. A very present help in times of trouble. Wow! I am sure that when we all look back over our lives and reflect on the times God protected us, all we can say is Wow! God is a good God; even when we are rebellious or disobedient, He is still loving us and loving on us. Even when I was disobedient to my parents and not doing what I was supposed to do, God was still good to me.

I cut Physical Education (PE) class an entire school year. The class was before my lunch period, so I would leave school and take two lunch breaks. That is how I encountered that creepy man in the first place because I was in a place where I was not supposed to be. After my mother reviewed my report card, she asked me why are you failing PE? I told her that I did not like to change clothes in front of the other girls and that the showers were too dirty; well, that was the end of that. My mom has always been a stickler about cleanliness, so she understood why I did not want to participate in PE. Well, wouldn't you know it; of course, I had to pass PE to graduate junior high school and that gym teacher gave me a hard time. She made me undress, shower, run, exercise, and participate in every aspect of PE. She made me pay for skipping her class the year before. Again, this was the consequence of my unwise choice to skip PE class, as well as that unfortunate incident on the way home.

Philippians 4:23 At the end of the apostle Paul's writing he would say: "The grace of our Lord Jesus Christ be with you all."

Well, that's my amazing testimony of great grace!

The grace of God has always been with me. Fast forward, I made it through high school by God's grace! Even though I was pregnant in my senior year, I finished high school before my son was born in August. By the grace of God, I enrolled in a career development school to help me prepare for the Civil Service Exam. I passed the Civil Service Exam and got a government job of which I proudly served forty years prior to retirement, all by the grace of God.

LESSON LEARNED:

Give God credit and be thankful for everything good that happens in your life, because it is only by His grace that you are living this very moment.

1 **Thessalonians 5:18** *"in everything give thanks; for this is the will of God in Christ Jesus for you."*

Luke 6:37 *"Judge not, and you shall not be judged. Condemn* *not, and you shall not be condemned. Forgive, and you will be forgiven."*

Please, don't judge Jay as a horrible human being. He was introduced into the drug game by our community, and his father was an illegal businessman himself, to put it mildly. When I was pregnant with our son, Jay expressed to me that his father told him that he needed to make his own money and provide for his own child. Jay was also a senior in high school as well, and he did not want to drop out of school, but the pressure to make money forced him to drop out of school. An unwise choice was made, on his part, and the beginning of a downward spiral in his life changed the trajectory of his life forever.

I do not desire, nor will I speak ill of the dead. Both Jay and his father have transitioned. My assignment herein is to share my experiences with Jay, and not focus on his father. Therefore, I will say that they both were complicated men, and the only reason I even mention Jay's father in this book is to explain how and why he started selling drugs. Once Jay got on the streets, he stepped onto the bad side. He had the women, the drugs, and money, as the song goes "Power Powder Respect" and I now, realize, that I allowed that behavior because I enjoyed the money and gifts he provided.

LESSON LEARNED.

A man will do to you what you allow him to do to you.

Now, if he really and truly loves you, he will respect you and honor and comply to your wishes. As we've heard Steve Harvey say, "men are simple" and I agree. If we women will set the tone of the relationship, the men will respect it –if they value the relationship. I finally saw and understood the error of my ways. I'm saying, it was my fault for not cutting Jay off but rather I tolerated Jay having all those women while I was in a relationship with him. The woman holds the cards because she holds the goods. So, ladies, know your worth.

UNDERSTANDING LOVE TYPES

Eros: Eros is the type of love that most closely resembles what Western cultures now view as romantic love. The word stems from the Greek word erotic, which translates to "intimate love."

Philia (Phileo): While many Greeks viewed eros as dangerous, they viewed philia as the ideal love. ... Philia refers to affection towards friends but is also used to refer to brotherly love.

Agape: Agape is a bit more abstract than the other two types of love. Agape is sometimes referred to in modern times as universal love, charity, or even altruism. Essentially, it's the love inside us that we give freely to others—regardless of our relationship to them. The whole idea of agape love is that we don't need to even have met the other person before, but we still want to help them, cooperate with them, or do good deeds towards them. While we may not expect anything in return for our selfless good deeds, studies show that they can actually benefit us—negating the effects of stress and having an overall positive affect on our mental health. Agape is also associated with God's unconditional love for all humanity.

The type of love I had for Jay was definitely Eros.

Eros plus the money, when the money was good, I enjoyed the fruits of Jay's labor. When the money was good, life was great, but the money was short-lived. Especially when Jay began to abuse his own products. He was carrying weapons and looking over his shoulders, and he was always acting weird, paranoid, and agitated. He was constantly saying that people were following him. These actions truly were red flags for me to get as far away from him as possible, but I was like Beyonce's song, "Crazy in Love".

Before Jay and I moved in together, one evening my mother came home early from work and caught us counting bags of money and stacking the money up on my bed. She told him to get his money and leave our house. My mother's home was not a place for that type of activity. My mother had higher expectations for me, and she did not like what was going on. Shortly after that incident, I moved out of the house and I moved in with him, which was yet another unwise choice.

Yes, we enjoyed the luxuries of that dirty money. We moved into his parents' townhouse, together, by age nineteen. I was so happy to finally have my man and child together in our own home, and I thought, this will show those women that I was number one in his life. We purchased some new furniture, went out to dinner all the time –oh we were living it up. Jay would bring cases of shrimp and lobster home and all types of valuable things people exchanged to purchase drugs. On many occasions he would take me to dinner, then to an early concert, bring me home, then he would leave out and take other women to the second show later that night. And by the next day, someone would call and tell me who they saw him out with. It got so bad, that I did not even confront him about it. Although I did not like it, I choose to turn my head, it was my unwise choice to stay in the relationship.

But within two weeks of living with him, I regretted in making the decision to move in together.

My mother tried to warn me, but once I turned nineteen

and had a baby, I thought I knew everything, but let me be clear –I was young and dumb! I sure learned the hard way, and the consequences of heartbreak and disappointments were devastating.

I came home early from work one day and there was another woman in our house. Some of the new furniture had not yet arrived, so they had a blanket on the living room floor. When I walked in, Jay was upstairs taking a shower and she was sitting on the blanket with her shoes off. *At a time like this, what do you do? Pray? What was I supposed to do? What would you have done?* I did not ask her any questions. I immediately jumped on her and started beating her. I must have blanked out for a moment. Jay heard the commotion, and he comes running down the stairs, so when he saw me whipping up on her, he grabs me, trying to hold me back saying, let her go, let her go. I had her by her long hair. I would not let her hair go. He kept saying, just let her go, let her go, so I finally let her hair go, and I turned around and I began hitting him, which I should have done in the first place. But right then and there I felt I needed to deal with her. I wanted her to experience what happens to you when you are in another woman's house, uninvited by the woman of the house, and you are with her man. She grabbed her shoes and ran out of the house. She hopped in her car and drove off. My girlfriend, who I call my big sister in our neighborhood, had blocked the woman's car in the space she had parked in so that I could catch them both together. My friend knew that I was going to take care of business once I got home. Once she was out of the house, I went upstairs and started throwing his clothes out of the bedroom window. I put him out of his own family's home. He just picked up his clothes, put them in his car, and left to give me time to cool off. That was an embarrassing moment. The neighbors were standing outside looking at me acting like a fool. Immediately, with everything inside of me, I wanted to move back home to my parents, but pride made me stay. I did not want to hear, I warned you. Once again, this was the consequence of an unwise choice. He was making more money than I at the time, and he was paying the rent, so within a week or so, I allowed him to return to the house, but when he returned, he was looking over his shoulders, for sure, because I was a woman scorned.

Jay gambled considerably, shooting dice with the neighborhood guys. One weekend his brothers came to visit him, so they were gambling with the guys on the streets. They got into a dispute over someone cheating. This incident caused Jay's brothers to get into a feud with a family in our neighborhood. Jay was already friends with these guys because they all hung out together, but now he was left to deal with them in a different light. This feud went on for a few days, and very quickly got out of control as they started shooting at each other. Jay attempted to shoot one of the guys in the head, but he said his gun was locked. Thank you, Jesus, for locking the gun. So, then Jay runs into the house, and the next thing I see, the house is surrounded by armed policemen, pointing their guns into the house, our house. This could have easily been another Breonna Taylor, story, which was about a 26-year-old African American woman who was fatally shot in her Louisville, Kentucky apartment on March 13, 2020. A similar situation for me because I was an innocent bystander. But God was protecting me. I opened the door and let them in. The officers came in searching the house and looking for weapons. In the meanwhile, someone had reached out to Jay's father, and he called while they were there, I answered the phone, and his father told me to ask the detective if they had a search warrant. When I asked, one detective gets so angry with me, he tells me to get off the phone, shut up and sit down. Of course, I complied immediately. I did not want to go to jail that night, or any night for that matter. They proceeded to search the house, and thankfully, they did not find a weapon. Jay denied (lying) having anything to do with the shoot-out incident in the neighborhood. But they still took him to the station for more questioning, and he got out of that situation. When I look back at that situation, and with the way police brutality is running rampant today, this situation could have gone another way because when I opened the door, police officers had their guns drawn. When I heard about the Breonna

Taylor incident, where shots were fired, fatally killing Breonna in her own home, while the police were looking for her boyfriend who, allegedly, was dealing in drugs, I could relate to her situation; that could have been me. To say the least, it was both unsafe and life-threatening in being in a relationship with Jay.

LESSON LEARNED:

Dating a drug dealer is not glamorous –like you see in the movies.

After a while, the money was never consistent, and it is never profitable unless the drug dealer is smart enough to invest their money into other businesses and get out of the game before it's too late. Jay never got to that point of investing because he ended up in prison.

Jay started getting arrested several times with drugs, and he finally had his day in court, and he eventually went to prison for a few years. I hated the prison scene. I was extremely nervous and uncomfortable going into prisons and I hated the search and pat-down process, with doors slamming behind me, the overcrowding, and those ghetto fabulous loud women. You saw where some of them were smuggling drugs into the prison and you could tell that some of the women did not wear underwear, because they were sitting on the guy's lap, always conducting themselves in an inappropriate manner in front of children. It was just a horrible scene and a degrading situation to be in. So, one would think, that this would be a good time to get out of the relationship, but no, I made the unwise choice to stay in the relationship and support him.

When Jay got transferred to a prison in West Virginia, in the mountains, which was like a college campus, it was a better environment – a better situation, and I did not mind going to that facility to visit him because it looked less intimidating. In West Virginia the inmates could dress in street clothes, he could wear sweatsuits and at this facility, he was able to complete his high school diploma and get his GED; he was even allowed to take some college courses, photography classes, and *voila!* Jay was doing better.

However, during one visit, I rode up with his mother (*referring to his mother as Ms. I*) Ms. I, and one of his friends. The visit was going quite well at first, and we were taking group pictures, but then before we left the facility, the friend who accompanied us on the visit went into the men's bathroom. He had brought some drugs into the facility for Jay, but as he was getting the drugs ready to give to Jay, he decides to use some of it. He got so high and then, he comes out of the bathroom with his zipper open and with his pants falling. He splattered water all over his face to get himself together, and he had a Jheri-curl hairstyle. Water was running down his face and with his hair dripping wet, he came out of that bathroom looking crazy, so the guards came over to us, questioning what was going on with him. I was so scared that they were going to arrest us, but we got out of there. Ms. I and I stepped up and explained to the guards that the guy was sick. Jay's mother was a quick thinker and a smooth operator; she remained cool and calm and got us out of that situation quickly. Yes, I love Ms. I; she was like a second mother to me. We had to ride back to Washington DC from West Virginia with this guy in the backseat, high on drugs. I remember us crowding up in the front seat. I never saw him again because he ended up getting killed months later after that incident.

When Jay was imprisoned, I became a single mom, and life was a struggle for us financially. I could not afford to keep the three-bedroom townhouse. So, I ended up moving into a one-bedroom apartment that was affordable. My son and I lived in the same apartment building as my auntie, in fact, we lived on the same floor, just across the hall from each other, which was a blessing, and just like when I was a little girl, I was back with my auntie again, and by this time, she was divorced, so it was a good living situation for us.

The lesson here is not to depend on people financially if they are not your spouse. And especially if they do not have a legitimate job. Because that person can roll out on you at any time. My momma taught me to be responsible. She told me to make sure that I pay my rent and car note before any other bills. She said, if I need food, gas, or household supplies, we can help, but it was my responsibility to provide for myself and my son, to keep a roof over our heads. I did take heed to that wise counsel, and it has proven, as I have never been evicted from any place I ever lived.

So, now, eventually, Jay returns home from prison, and he gets a job, but he does not keep it for long because the streets were calling him. And this time, he starts smoking crack cocaine. Now before crack, he initially smoked marijuana and snorted cocaine, but the crack epidemic had hit the streets of Washington DC. It was a cheaper drug and more attainable. Eventually, and unfortunately, Jay got addicted to smoking crack. He started staying away from the house for several days at a time. Women he associated with in the streets started smoking crack cocaine along with him. Still, I did not leave him.

I did not like that he used drugs, sold drugs, and had other women in his life, but since I was not willing to assist him in the street life, I felt there was nothing I could do about his choices. I simply set up boundaries for my safety however, I did put up with his bad behavior. I told Jay to never bring drugs around me or stash them in my house. I guess he did not believe me, because one day I found a bag of white powder hidden in a closet. I was so nervous, but I undeniably flushed the whole bag of powder down the toilet. I paged him for hours, but he did not reply to my page, so when he returned home and saw that those drugs were gone, both he and his brothers were upset with me. They asked me why I didn't page one of them to come to pick it up? I did not answer them directly, first, I did not know to whom that powder belonged, secondly, I told Jay not to have drugs around me or my son, so I replied that I am not going to jail for any of you. I reminded Jay that I told him not to stash drugs in my house and I meant it. I was serious and clear about those boundaries. I put them all on notice to keep their shady business away from me, my son, our home. I never had any problems with any of them from that point forward. I was serious about protecting my child, my freedom as well as our livelihood because I never knew when Jay would get arrested and go back to prison.

Once again, a man will only do what you allow him to do. It was already dangerous, with people thinking he had money, he and his brothers had gotten robbed before. They had targets on their backs. Three of his brothers ended up being murdered; two of the brother's cases were over twenty years old – cold cases, where they disappeared, and no one knew what happened to them. That story would be another book project.

Unfortunately, for them, the consequences of unwise choices.

Situations and circumstances upon situations and circumstances, I was slowly getting the message that Jay was not going to be the normal "nine to five" type of guy or the father his son deserved. He put us in dangerous situations many times, by carrying guns, large amounts of money –large amounts of money of which I could not explain if I got caught with him dropping off money to people. One time, Jay got stopped, and he had outstanding tickets he had not paid, and there was a warrant out for him, but the police let him go because we were in the car with him. He told Jay to take care of those tickets right away. These grave life experiences with Jay were certainly something to remember, and I finally realized, not worth it. The bad times surely outweighed the good times. *Remember readers*: Money cannot buy you, love.

LESSON LEARNED:

When a man puts your life and your child's life in various kinds of risks, he is not worth the risks. If he really loves you, he will never put you in compromised positions, and being naïve is not an excuse.

THE FINAL BREAK UP.

I found a woman's address on a utility bill in one of Jay's pockets. I drove over to the address, with my child in the car with me. When we got to the apartment complex, I was looking for the building and my son who was only five years old says, *no mommy, he pointed and said, it's the building over there.* Jay had been taking our son to her house. Both my son and I got out of the car and we both go into the building; I knocked on her door. When the lady opened the door, and I saw who she was, I was furious! Then she says in a nasty tone, what do *you* want? I could not say anything, or even think clearly, I just pushed her back into *her* apartment. Jay runs out of the bedroom and comes out into the hall. Here we go again, and now I am going into someone else's personal space to fight. I grabbed him and preceded to pull him down the stairs. I was so angry; somehow, I gained strength from within! I was tired of him cheating on me. The neighbors began to come out of their apartments because of course, we were making a big scene. Someone shouted to someone to call the police. I believe this is when I snapped out of my rage! Here I am, coming to her apartment starting trouble and with my son with me. So, my son and I returned to my car, but before I got in the car, I saw a big rock; I picked up the rock and I was just about to bust out his car window, but then he picked up a rock and said, if you break out my windshield, I am going to break yours.

I thought twice about that and dropped the rock, got into my car, and drove away. He jumped in his car, and he follows me to our apartment; then she gets her brother to bring her over to our apartment. She knew where we lived. Who knows if she had been in our apartment! I went into my aunt's apartment across the hall, and I told her what had just happened. My auntie said, y'all ladies need to confront him –not each other. When I went in the hallway of the building, she was there, so both of us cornered him, he started backing up towards the steps, he turns around and ran down the stairs, and out of the building. When we backed him up in a corner, he ran like a coward. We all were standing there; my auntie said, *"You both need to leave him alone because he is playing you both."* We ended up coming inside my apartment and we set down and talked like civilized women. We agreed to leave him alone. He called each one of us later that night to apologize, stating he would leave the other alone. I told him to leave me alone, I kept my end of the bargain. A day or so later when I spoke to the other woman, she said, he came back to her, and they made up and they were going to work things out, together. At this point, you would think that would be the end of my life story with him. Well, no, no, no –not yet.

He comes back and says he is going to be committed to me, and he asked me to marry him. We go to the courthouse to get our marriage license. I begin to plan a wedding. I thought I finally got the man that I loved since I was thirteen. During the process of planning the wedding, Ms. I suggested that we just go to the Justice of the Peace and get married. She wanted us to get married right away. But I did not understand the urgency. I wanted to have a church wedding. I did not see a reason to rush. But herein again, I discovered that Jay was still seeing the other woman, and yep! *they* ended up going to the Justice of the Peace and *yep*, they got married –married to each other. On the day they got married, he came to the apartment real early that morning to see me, while I was still in bed. Thinking back, now, I realized he was coming to tell me that he was getting married. But instead, he gets into bed with me. A few hours later, I started getting ready for work and when I walked out the bathroom he was gone. It seemed odd that he did not say a word, but I was in a rush to get to work. That evening, I did not hear anything from him, which wasn't strange. The next day Ms. I called while I was at work. She said she was coming over that evening to talk to me about something important. When she arrived at my apartment, she informed me that Jay had gotten married the day before. I was shocked, traumatized, bewildered, deceived, brokenhearted, and everything else you can name; he was just with me that very morning, and now, he is married!!! Who does that! I mean, who would do that! I could not believe it! I took days off from work because I could not concentrate on my work, nor could I sleep. I felt hopeless and depressed. Wondering how he could betray me, especially doing something like this! We had been together for ten years of my life –well I was with him ten years of my life; he was never really with just me. We had a son together, but a child will not help you keep a man. But fortunately, him getting married was the biggest blessing in my life. God was looking out for me. His wife did not win the prize, because he took her through continual distress, pain, anguish, and torment, with the drug addiction, and their toxic marriage; they ended up divorcing. He was back knocking at my door two weeks after he got married. Asking me to let him in because he wanted to see his son, after midnight. But thank God for Ms. I! I called her, and she said, do not let him in, he made his choice, and now he had to live with it. Ms. I was hurt about him not even telling her that he was going to get married, but she was there for me, and she helped me during a very difficult time in my life. She encouraged me by giving me a scripture to read every day and I recited scriptures daily until it came alive in my life.

Proverbs 3:5 *"Trust in the Lord with all your heart, lean not unto your own understanding, in all your ways acknowledge Him, and He shall direct your path."*

This scripture gave me hope for the future. I wrote it out on a piece of paper taped it on my bedroom dresser mirror and bathroom mirror. I read it every morning and evening for months. Until it penetrated my heart and soul and gave me peace. Just like that scripture helped me to heal, the scriptures helped me to forgive. I was grateful we did not get married. He went into a drug program, and he eventually re-dedicated his life to Christ. But he struggled with drug addiction off and on for years. He remarried but unfortunately, that marriage ended in divorce as well. He asked me to forgive him for all the hurt, pain, and humiliation he caused me, and I did. He reconciled his relationship with our son. We ended up being the best of friends before he transitioned.

LESSON LEARNED:

Forgiveness

Jay did not have an easy life, he had lots of struggles, addictions, and demons to fight. He repented and he apologized to me serval times for the way things turned out and I forgave him because my forgiving him was for me. When he got sick, he moved back home with Ms. I, and when I would call her, he would answer the phone and we would talk for a while, and he would tell me just how proud of me he was that I was in ministry. Redemption is powerful.

Ephesians1:7 *"In whom we have redemption through his blood, the forgiveness of sins, according to the riches of his grace;"*

As Jesus forgave me of my sins, I choose to forgive Jay!

Forgiveness heals and forgiveness can set us free.

May Jay rest in peace.

CHAPTER 3

*Situationship #2 - Out of the Frying Pan into the
Fire*

*"The righteous choose their friends carefully, but the way of the
wicked leads them astray."* **Proverbs 12:26** (NIV)

I met Mr. G through his business relationship with Jay's
family years earlier. He was a handsome light-skin
brother, light brown eyes, wavey hair, well dressed –a
pretty boy if you will. A teachable moment, the Bible
says:

1 John 2:16 *"For everything in the world-the lust of the flesh, the
lust of the eyes, and the pride of life—comes not from the Father
but from the world."*

Consequently, I learned the hard way that looks are
deceiving. Although physical attraction may be the first
connection, we must not allow it to be the only
connection. We should try to get to know the person as
much as possible, for example, first and foremost, find
out about their faith, their belief, their upbringing, their
family, their education, and last, but certainly not least,

their goals in life. These are the qualities that will help you realize if this person is a good fit for you. There are some fine-looking men and women in this world who will catch your eyes, but they could, unfortunately, be on drugs, incarcerated, in debt, bad credit, on the down-low (on the quiet; in secret: concealing their true homosexuality); infected with diseases, womanizers, prostitutes and so on. They may not believe in the God you serve; for me, it's God the Father, God the Son (Jesus), and God the Holy Spirit. So, it is important to get to know a person first.

At that time, all I learned of Mr. G was that he was handsome, very flashy, and loved to dress; he was that dude (back in the day) who was known in certain parts of Washington DC at the go-go's dancing, and he loved being seen, and he also had a great sense of humor. A man who could make women laugh can be attractive in and by itself. My view at the time was that if a man can make me laugh, he has a good chance to win my heart. I guess you could say I had a secret crush on Mr. G years before we ever dated. When I would see him around the city, I would say to myself, he is so fine. On many occasions, I would see him at different places around Washington DC, concerts at Constitution Hall, and the Warner Theater, and when a new movie came out, I would run into him at different movie theaters. Mr. G sold drugs for Jay's family business, so he was everywhere.

I befriended him and exchanged numbers so that I would have an inside person, a PI (private investigator) to know what Jay was up to (this was the period when Jay and I were still together) as far as other women were concerned and where he would frequent. So eventually I got Mr. G to confide in me because he knew where and with whom Jay was hanging out.

Men think women are stupid, however, the fact is that men are stupid for thinking women are stupid. Most women are one step ahead of men and I'd like to think this of me. Well, unfortunately, during this time, while Jay was cheating on me, I was also cheating on him, but he never caught me cheating on him. News flash! I was not as naïve as Jay thought. I was trying to get information out of Mr. G, and we, well, we just vibe together. So, we hooked up and went out one night. But Washington DC is so small because we went to the movies all the way uptown and still ran into someone we knew from the southeast area. The girl we ran into told Mr. G's "baby momma" that she saw us at the movies. Somehow, she got a hold of my phone number, and I don't know how, but anyway, she called accusing me of messing around with her man; she also threatened to come over to my side of town to beat me up. However, when I did not back down from her threats, (remember the bully lesson in Chapter 1) she began to talk to me like she had some common sense. Yes, I did deny that anything was going on and by the time we finished our conversation, we were friend-enemies, (meaning friendly but really an enemy). That was my last conversation with her so after that situation and our conversation, I left him alone until years later. I was able to get out of that situation without Jay knowing anything about it; as far as I knew, he wasn't aware of it because he never confronted me about it. Jay was dating one of her girlfriends at the time. She was this" fly chick" beautiful and well dressed from New York City but she was nothing more than a female hustler, who ran circles around Jay, she was a few years older and a lot more street wiser than he. Actually, he was out of her league in the first place. Mr. G provided me the information about the lady, therefore, after that incident with "baby mama" we never spoke again, until years later because Mr. G was eventually incarcerated so we totally lost contact (hereinafter, called "G" in the remainder of this chapter).

Years later, when G got out of prison Jay had been married and moved on with his life. And I was dating a guy from my church. He was not my type; just another handsome face and he was someone nice who paid attention to me, during the time I needed attention, but he was a bit of a momma's boy, kind of immature (he would tease my son and make him mad), and if you know me, you knew not to mess with my children. Really, he was just someone to help me get over the pain and embarrassment of being jilted by Jay. The church boy was worth mentioning because I ended up breaking his heart when I dropped him like a hot potato and started dating G. This is when I learned "hurting people, hurt people". I did not mean to hurt him. I was just trying to survive my own personal trauma.

Anyway, I ran into G's god-sister (who was another one of Jay's ladies, we all knew each other). And she mentioned that G was getting out of prison soon. I told her to let him know that I asked about him and to give him my phone number when he was released. A few months later after that conversation, G gave me a call. When we talked, he told me that he was out of the game and that he was going to get his life together, get a job and be legitimate. But what he did not tell me was that he was addicted to heroin. I had no idea about his heroin addiction, unknowingly to me, he had been addicted to drugs for years. Me being gullible, I knew nothing about heroin. So, when he said, he was going to be legitimate, I took his word at face value because I wanted it to be true, no questions asked. I did not make him prove himself to be a legitimate man and genuine or true to his word. I jumped right into dating him. I guess you would call it, "right out of the frying pan into the fire". What was I thinking! Within six months of our relationship (the honeymoon phase), I got pregnant. I did not plan to have a baby with him, but now that I was pregnant, (although it was a financial strain), I planned to keep my new blessing, because every life is a blessing.

Right after discovering I was pregnant, I started noticing negative things about him. I grew very concerned about him because he would nod off quite a bit and he had bruises on his arm, –I was so naïve! I thought the bruises were passion marks on his arm, not bruises from a drug needle, and the biggest sign was that he would stay in the bathroom for hours at a time. One evening we were going out to dinner for his birthday, and he said he needed to stop at a friend's house. We go into this neighborhood uptown Washington DC, and G says that he would be right back. I told him to please hurry because I was uncomfortable sitting out there in the car in this neighborhood. He left me sitting in that car for over three hours. I was so scared, and I did not have the keys to the car, so I could not move it, and it was getting dark. All types of drug addicts, drug dealers, prostitutes, and homeless people were walking up and down the street. When he finally came out of that building, he was staggering to the car. I cursed him out and demanded he take me home. I told him that I was done with him. From the way he was acting, it became very clear to me that he was shooting up heroin. I did not talk to him for a month after that incident.

Then one day I finally told him that I thought I was

pregnant. He was so excited, that he went to the doctor's office with me to confirm it. He said he was going to get himself together, but it never happened on my watch. There is nothing good about being addicted to drugs; drugs will destroy a person's life and it also leads to an early death. A few times G came over and took me to my doctors' appointments (during my pregnancy), and he would see to it that I had food, vitamins, and things I needed, but he kept nodding off (dosing off) which was embarrassing to me in public, people looking at him. I could not deal with that, so I stopped him from coming around me totally because I was very uncomfortable being around him. I went through my pregnancy alone. I did not see him or communicate with him for months until the day I was in labor, and that ended up being a big disaster.

Okay, so I worked up until the day before I delivered my beautiful healthy baby girl. It was a Friday evening when I started going into labor. When I got off work that day, I took my son who was seven years old, and his cousin to their karate lesson at June Reed Studio on St. Barnabas Rd. in Maryland. My son's instructor was this young guy who flirted with me throughout my entire pregnancy. God blessed me with beauty, and a smile, even during this pregnancy, I was still getting attention from men while carrying my little one. Fast forward, I ended up marrying that karate instructor, and that "situationship" is in the next chapter!

Anyways, while I was waiting for the karate lesson to be over; my back began to hurt so bad that I could hardly sit still, and I literally could not wait until the lesson was over. Once the lesson was over, we got out of there, picked up a pizza, and headed home for the evening. By midnight, I was having contractions every couple of hours. I would then go into the bathroom and take a hot shower and lie back down. By 5:00 am Saturday morning, I was in full labor. It was time to head to the hospital. To this day, I still do not know why I called G, but I did so to let him know that I was in labor and that I was heading to the hospital as soon as my father arrives at my apartment because he would drive me to the hospital, and he would also watch the boys. G and my father arrived at my apartment around the same time; in fact, G walked to my apartment. My dad drives us to the hospital; we check-in, and a doctor immediately examined me and stated that I had not dilated enough; and that I needed to go back home for a few more hours. But before I could get dressed, my water broke so I was then admitted, and I was only in the labor room for two hours before I delivered my baby. It was a smooth delivery, fast and everything went well. G was there in the delivery room with me, so he got to see her birth. She was so beautiful! She had a head full of curly dark hair, and most importantly, she was healthy. However, I was genuinely concerned about both my health as well as my baby because of G's heroin addiction and him potentially sharing needles. I was afraid that we might have contracted HIV or some other incurable disease, and yes, I did inform my doctor of G's situation. My doctor ordered every type of blood test possible for any and every disease imaginable. All test results returned negative –with good reports so we were both good, so I had to give a shout of praise to my God! "Thank You, Jesus!" God's protection covered us.

But hold on, the story gets worse before it gets better. By this time, at my weakest point after having a baby, I gave G my purse and my overnight bag to take to my hospital room, and what happens next will shock you. G steals my money and keys out of my purse. Keys to my car, apartment, and my aunt's apartment (who lived across the hall from me). Once I am transported to my hospital room, G and my father left so that I could get some rest. My father gives G a ride to his apartment building. When my father drops him off, G doubles back and walks to my apartment. He breaks into my aunt's apartment and steals her VCR while she was in her bedroom, asleep. This all happened on my aunt's birthday, which was the same day as my daughter's birth; my aunt had been celebrating all night. Fortunately, she did not hear him creeping around in her apartment. He was totally strung out on heroin and in need of money for a fix. I could not imagine what would have happened to my auntie if she would have awakened while he was robbing her. The crazy thing about this story was that he had purchased a new VCR for me, and no one was in my apartment so why would he break into her apartment and steal from her, which was beyond my comprehension. But this lets you know he was in a confused and desperate state of mind. Who breaks into someone's home while they are sleeping in the next room, unhooks their VCR, and locks up the person's apartment! I had some fine jewelry, watches, stereos, and TVs in my apartment that he could have moved quickly. I would have felt better if he would have gone into my apartment and stolen my stuff, instead of my aunt's possessions. He had already stolen my keys and the money in my purse. And of course, he took my car.

So there, you see, he was out on the streets robbing people while using my car. When my aunt wakes up later that day and notices her VCR missing, she immediately calls the police. They came over to take the report from her. She told them I lived across the hall from her, and I had keys to her apartment but that I was in the hospital. She explained to them that I had just delivered a baby early that morning. They called me and asked if my keys were missing? When I checked my purse, yep, of course, they were gone. I asked if my car was parked in the lot, and my car was gone, so we knew it was him. The police still came up to the hospital to verify our story and asked me questions about G, because they had gotten a call about a robbery with the description of my car. I was so nervous my blood pressure shot to the roof. I was depressed, embarrassed, and humiliated about this whole situation. Now my family would know he was a stone-cold junky, a thief and he had both our house keys out there doing who knows what! My aunt had our locks changed by the time we returned home from the hospital. The next day, my baby brother, and my cousin, who lived in the same area where G lived and hung out, went looking for G to get my car back. They drove around the neighborhood and found him. My baby brother approached G and obtained my keys without incident and returned my car to me safely. Of course, G had some of his items in my car: a big club and some of his drug paraphernalia. My baby brother was kind enough to clean my car out before returning it to me. We then reported to the police that we got the car back.

Once discharged from the hospital a couple of days later, one of the police officers comes to my apartment to let us know that G was apprehended and was being held at the District of Columbia Jail. The officer wanted us to file charges against him and take him to court. But I was so depressed, that I did not have the energy or mental capacity to deal with it. I just could not do it. The officer was discussing the situation with me, and suddenly, I immediately break down, crying profusely. The officer suggested that I seek advice from a therapist. I felt so depressed after all of this. My auntie would come over to get my daughter and keep her all day long, while I slept. I stayed in bed for a couple of weeks. I felt as if I had gotten myself into the worst situation than I was with Jay. Hooking up with G was the most unwise, unhealthy decision I had ever made, and as I thought this situation through, it was all my fault because I pursued him from the very beginning, when I gave his god-sister my phone number to give to him.

G went away to prison, but before he would be sent away, he was held at the Washington DC Jail, and after what he did to me, he still called me from the facility, mind you, collect! And yes, your girl answered the phone. I wanted answers to why would he do such a horrible thing to my auntie? Why didn't he just take the VCR and other valuable gifts he had given me? He initially apologized, and said, he would make sure he replaced what he had stolen. He told me that he was sick and was not thinking clearly. Then he asked about our daughter and wanted to see her before his sentencing and before he was sent away. I felt so sorry for him, and I felt a pressing in my heart to visit him in jail. All the while I am praying that his eyes would open from darkness into God's marvelous light. Perhaps God placed me in G's path that he may turn away from demonic strongholds and turn to the power and strength of Almighty God. I believe that by me forgiving him, and showing up for him with acts of kindness, allowing him to see his daughter after what he did to me on the day that she was born, he would see the unconditional love and the kind of mercy God gives us when He sent Jesus to die for our sins.

However, as I see it, I received a sweet blessing out of the relationship with him; I have a beautiful daughter, a loving son-in-law, and four wonderful grandsons to continue our family legacy. God truly turned a hopeless mess of a situation into a blessing.

Acts 26:18 *"To open their eyes, and to turn them from darkness to light, and from the power of Satan unto God, that they may receive forgiveness of sins, and inheritance among them which are sanctified by faith that is in me."*

Always striving to be the bigger person in a relationship, and striving to show the love of God, I decided to take my baby to that dirty DC jail so that G could see her. I did not tell anyone, because I was too ashamed and embarrassed to let anyone know that I visited him in jail; actually, I don't think anyone would have understood why I would take my baby to see him; I feared that they would criticize me even more than they already had. Still, through it all, I knew my Heavenly Father was with me and for me – unconditionally, and because God was with and for me, I have always had compassion for the loss – the unsaved and I always cheer for the underdog. Christ loved me so much. Even when I was in the world, God demonstrated His love toward me. The following scripture was key in changing the way I viewed God, and it re-affirms to me just how much God loves me.

Romans 5:8 *"But God commended His love toward us, in that, while we were yet sinners, Christ died for us."*

When you know this kind of love, you can give this kind of love. All throughout the New Testament, we see Jesus' expressions of compassion toward the loss, the outcasts, the poor, and the sick, and since we are created in His image and likeness, as Jesus is, so are we in this world. And if we could learn to look at people like God does when He sent His only begotten Son into the world to be an atonement for our sins, we would not hold unforgiveness towards our brothers and sisters. Although God loves all humanity, no matter who you are, it's the sin that He frowns upon, because God is Holy.

1 Peter 1:16 *"because it is written, Be Holy, for I am Holy."*

God desires all His children to find their way to the light –His light; Jesus is the way, the truth, and the life as well as the light.

John 14:6 (KJV) *"Jesus saith unto him, I am the way, the truth, and the life: no man cometh unto the Father, but by me."*

We can search high, and we can search low, and we will

never find anyone greater than our God. No relationship could ever compare to the love of God.

While dating G, I discovered that he practiced the Muslim or Islam, religion, however, before he transitioned, he did accept Jesus as his personal Lord and Savior, and he joined a Christian church. I truly believe that by sharing my faith, ministering to him, and showing him God's love, even after he committed the robbery against me and my family — and I still befriended him as a friend, and I believe it touched his heart.

After that visit with my baby to the Washington DC jail, G and I never saw each other again until our daughter was about three years old. I had gotten married, divorced already, and moved to El Paso, TX, and then back to Washington, DC again during the time he was incarcerated.

When he was released from prison, G got a work release position on the Flag Ship Cruise Boat, local lunch and dinner cruise ship at the Waterfront in southeast Washington DC, and as he promised, he paid my auntie for the VCR he had previously stolen. I took our daughter to meet him one evening after he got off work, we were waiting at the dock. She was afraid of him, and she would not allow him to touch her or allowed me to put her down. So, I held her for the entire visit. But nonetheless, G was smiling, and grateful that I would allow him to see her again.

Honestly, I had no plans to reach out to him. When he contacted me, the reason I introduced her to him was due to a colleague telling me a story about her family situation. She was raised to believe that her brother was her cousin. Her uncle adopted her brother and raised him as his own son. And when the uncle died, the truth came out. She shared how that situation damaged both her and her brother, deeply. They were hurt and angry with their relatives for keeping a secret from them. Her experience both alarmed me and touched me. I did not want my daughter to be devastated by a lie thinking my ex-husband was her biological father. My colleague's story impacted me. I decided to tell my daughter the truth about who her biological father was. And this was the reason I took her down to that ship to meet her biological father. It took several years before she was finally comfortable being around him alone. As she grew older, he would come and pick her up from time to time and she would always take her baby brother along with her. She was in high school by the time G got married and he asked her to participate in his wedding. That is when they really began to bond. G also had a younger son from another relationship. And they all made up for lost time; it was nice to see them all bonding together.

As I stated earlier, G did accept Christ and he converted to Christianity. They seemed to be coming along well, together, as a family for a few years, and then, unfortunately, he slipped back into darkness. He relapsed and began to use drugs again; they lost everything, even the marriage. After that, he was estranged from our daughter once again. Our daughter saw him one day as she was driving home. He was crossing the street in front of her car, and he looked depraved and dirty. She told me that she could not move and that she was shocked to see him in this condition. All she could do was stare at him as he walked right by her car, and she couldn't even speak to him. It was shocking, hurtful, both sad and pitiful (she felt a ball of emotions); he had reached rock bottom. When she got married, she invited him to her wedding. He asked her if he was walking her down the aisle, and she said no, rather he was an invited guest. So yes, G came to the wedding, but for some reason, he did not stay; it appeared that he left the wedding before she walked down the aisle. He did not even see her in her beautiful wedding gown. I believe he was hurt that she did not want him to walk her down the aisle because she wanted her big brother and her stepfather (my current husband) to walk her down the aisle and give her away. Unfortunately, they never spoke again. The next time she saw him, he was in the hospital, and in a coma. He died the very next day after that visit and although he never provided for her, she made his funeral arrangements, along with her siblings. In all of this, she forgave her father. I try to teach my children by my example of forgiving others, to forgive, forgiveness is for you.

Matthew 6:15 *"But if you do not forgive men their trespasses, neither will your Father forgive your trespasses."*

I wanted them to understand that if they can't forgive others, how can they expect God to forgive their sins.

LESSON LEARNED:

Message to absentee fathers: When you make decisions or choices to abandon your child/children, (for whatever reasons) there will be consequences of your unwise choices.

You would do well to not get mad or angry at your child/children for not including you in their special moments and accomplishments in life. When special occasions come about or happen, you must not be surprised; you should understand that they may not choose you to be involved. They will most likely choose the person who was there for them. Therefore, you cannot blame them for your absences, so, own up to your choices no matter what your reasons are for being absent. After all, they had to navigate through life without you. If you don't want to reap the negative feelings when you are left out, be there for your children, and I stress, no matter what situation you are in. Unfortunately, in my daughter's situation, she and G never had the chance to have a conversation concerning his feelings or disappointment for not walking her down the aisle on her special day.

This chapter ends sadly because they never got to speak, have an understanding, closure, or clear things up between them. Some people think they have time to make things right, but we never know the day or the hour when we transition to the next dimension of life, therefore, it is imperative that we forgive one another.

Ephesians 6:4 *"And you, fathers, do not provoke your children to wrath but bring them up in the training and admonition of the Lord."* AMEN

CHAPTER 4

Situationship #3 - The Karate Instructor

"They profess to know God, but in works they deny Him, being abominable, disobedient, and disqualified for every good work."
Titus 1:16

In Chapter 3, I made mention of the karate instructor who would flirt with me from time to time during my pregnancy with my daughter. Let's call him K, for karate. K really was not the one for me. First, he was five years younger than me and very immature. Although he was attracted to me (in my pregnancy state) I was not attracted to him. He was not a handsome man in my opinion, but he had a nice personality, his athleticism –he held a black belt in karate, and he was an instructor. He told me that he was a spiritual person and that he believed in God. We connected for two reasons; he gave me attention when I needed it the most, and my son liked him. On one occasion, while in the car, leaving my son's karate class, my son expressed how much he liked K and how he wished K was his father. For those two reasons, I entertained the idea of getting to know K. Soon after our meeting and my son's classes, shortly thereafter K enlisted in the Army and ended up with orders to, be stationed in El Paso Texas. We did stay in contact with each other as he would call often to check up on me and my family. He was charming and appeared to be a good, decent man.

One day, he called to see how everything was going with me and said that he was coming home for the Christmas holiday and that we should get together. So, when he came home to visit it was like *Stella getting her groove back* concerning me, and I now saw him in a different light; I was then attracted to him, and he became very handsome to me. By New Year's Eve, before he left to return to duty, he asked me to marry him and for me and my family to relocate to El Paso. I was tired of the way my life was going in Washington DC, and even though I was not in love with him, I said, yes. I saw this as an opportunity for me to get away from Washington, DC, and to make a new start in life with my two children. I also thought about the military benefits, continuing my career in the Federal government, and traveling around the world. I had been in love and had lost, so I thought love will grow in time, so why not step out on faith, and take a risk. And five months later, we were married. He came back twice within our five-month engagement period, and he gave me a five-karat, beautiful diamond ring. As well as being a little on the flashy side, he was consistently loving and kind, so life was delightful, and I was indeed hopeful for a positive change.

Sidebar: Oh, I should mention that I did see a red flag before we got married. I had received a warning from one of his old girlfriends. One morning I was leaving home for work, and this young lady approached me in front of my apartment building. She stated her name and said she was his former girlfriend and that they had recently broken up because she wouldn't marry him. She shared with me that she felt he needed to grow up some more, that he was irresponsible, that he had bad credit, and that he was pursuing a wife only because he was having a difficult time adjusting to being in the military, and he had no family while stationed in El Paso, plus the military pay more money for families. At the time, I believed that she was being truthful with me, but I was looking at this five-karat diamond ring on my finger and I surmised that she was just jealous (you know how we think sometimes), because how could he afford to buy me this ring if he had bad credit? Anyway, I thought to myself, *well, I did not know her, so why would I trust her?* Then I started thinking of his stepmother, that she must have put her up to doing this because K's stepmother did not approve of him marrying me. She must have given the young lady my name and address; someone had to. This was a few weeks before the wedding. So, I quickly dismissed her.

Our wedding was simply beautiful. The honeymoon in the Pocono's was fantastic. Everything was going well and all of life was now in a good place. Also, I had submitted my paperwork with my employer, scheduled my last day at work, with authorization to transfer to a new job on the military base where we lived comfortably, with an effort to save financially — so it was all good. So, I was not about to drop my plans for some random chick who appeared to be either jealous or envious of us getting married. Perhaps if I would have listened to her, I would have saved myself from the consequences of more drama, and trauma in my life. Also, on several occasions before the marriage, his stepmother had tried to discourage me as well. She was rude in the manner in which she spoke to me, and when I told her that I was still going to marry K, she was furious with me. But she still supported us and attended the wedding. I guess she initially saw me as an opportunist and now, as I looked back on the entire situation, she was not wrong. I had enough of Washington DC, so I thought perhaps if I relocate to another area, my life will get better.

I do not regret the experience of living in El Paso, and I meant no harm to anyone. I was trying to heal and better my life in the best way possible, and since he gave me an opportunity to do so I took him up on his offer. It may have seemed that I was using him, but I felt as if it was a two-way street in this situation because he was using me as well. He was lonely and wanted to have a family to support him during his tour. Initially, things were great, and we all were adjusting well. K was a hopeless romantic and he knew how to "woo you". He was the kind of guy who brought flowers home to me and we would have date night on Fridays. It did not take long for me to fall in love with him. This kind of love I will categorize as *Pragma* love; pragma love is the Greek word for, "shopping list love". Pragma is love based on duty, practical reasons, and shared goals. Like Philia, Pragma is not limited to romantic partnerships, although it is a vital part of romantic love. It is essential within families and even close friendships. You see, K supplied my needs for a season. He constantly asked me if I was homesick, and I would say no. I just wanted and needed a change. He was expecting me to be sad, and he knew that I missed my relatives and my best girlfriend. We cried like babies prior to my leaving Washington DC. She was so mad at him for taking me away, and to add insult to injury, he was laughing at us crying like babies. Honestly, I was happy to be away from all the drama I was experiencing in Washington, DC.

I met the neighbors quickly and made friends easily. They were from all over the world; very different people from the normal friends and associates I had in Washington DC. K would have to go out in the fields for weeks at a time, and it did not bother me at all. One Friday night he came home unexpectedly from the field, and I had a house full of military wives. We were drinking wine, eating, laughing –just having some fun and enjoying ourselves. K was shocked and seemed upset that I had no problem adjusting to my new life and making friends. Poor thing did not even know that I was good with or without him being home; I was enjoying my new environment. I felt safe living on a military base. The base was safer than the streets of Washington DC, and I knew how to handle myself. I had a car. I had new friends who knew the area. I had a new job. We found a nice church on base that we attended regularly. I felt complete with my new life, but nonetheless, it was short-lived.

Unfortunately, adverse situations started happening, that is, experiencing an environment of systemic racism, while living on the base with other cultures.

One day my son was playing with the neighborhood children, which he did frequently. They were a diverse group of kids — mixed cultures, Black, White, Hispanic, etc. On this one occasion, my son was play-fighting with another kid, and with my son's knowledge and experience with karate, he knew some neat karate moves. He kicked a white kid in the groin area, and of course, the kid went home crying to his dad. The father came to our house upset, and while outside, he came up to my son and grabbed him by the collar and said, "*Boy, you better not ever put your hands on my son again or I will kick your butt."* (Actually, I'm being polite herein –not wanting to use the words he used.) I heard commotion going on outside and I heard what the father said so I walked out on the porch, and I asked the father who he was talking to. My son then told me what happened and that the man had grabbed his shirt! I was like, WHAT! I yelled at the man and told him that he didn't know who he was messing with, and that I was going to tell my husband what he did, and my husband is going to kick his butt. The neighbor immediately returned to his house. Shortly thereafter as I turned to go back into my house to call my husband, my husband pulls up to our house right on time. We told him what had just happened. K took my son by the hand and told me to go into the house and calm down because, now at this time, I am pregnant with K's child. Of course, I did not listen to him but instead I followed them both to the neighbor's house, with me fussing all the way, *saying "nobody was gonna put their hands on my child".*

When we get to the neighbor's house, there were four other white guys sitting on his porch (it appeared that they were all playing cards), their wives and other children were sitting out there with them. K walked up to the neighbor's porch; he asked my son to identify which one grabbed him. Then K addressed the man in a calm tone and asked the neighbor to explain to him what happened. The neighbor started yelling about his son having a hernia and that my son kicked him in the groin or affected area. K began explaining that boys play-fight all the time, and of course, no one knew of his son's medical condition. Then K asked the man did he grabbed our son. But before the man could answer, I blurted out, *"Yes, he grabbed him and threatened him, and that he does not know who he is messing with."* So that man turned to my husband and said, "You need to tell that B to shut up!" Why did he say that! K punched the man in the nose, broke his nose, and put him into a headlock, choking him. Everyone started screaming and while this was going on, the other guys did not make a move. As K was choking the guy, I saw that the man was blacking out, so I went over to K very slowly and tapped him on the shoulder, saying, let him go, please let him go. K dropped the headlock and the man dropped to the porch. We simply turned around and walked away.

Shortly, right after the altercation, the Military Police (MP) showed up at our home. The MP took both men in for questioning and to write up a formal incident report. But neither of them was criminally charged concerning the incident because they both handled the situation wrong. Unfortunately, it was me not listening to K (to go back into the house) which escalated the incident. Again, I stand by my saying that the neighbor should not have put his hands on my child and disrespected me —calling me out of my name. I know the situation was handled immaturely, as I was only twenty-seven and K was only twenty-two at the time. K did attempt to handle the situation in an orderly fashion, but I was responsible for that situation getting out of control. As I think back, I do believe we were the only black family on that street, but from that time until we moved, we had no more problems with anyone on that street. They knew not to mess with us.

On Friday evenings, before my pregnancy was beginning to show, we would go out to dinner as a family. Later in the evening, after dinner, K and I would get a sitter for the kids, and we would go to the NCO Club, which was only one street over from our house. When K walked into the club, the guys would be lined up against the wall and they would give him a dap, or a high five like he was a celebrity. Oh, and remember early on that I mentioned dancing was my thing, (we both were great dancers), so we became very popular, and we were known as the Washington DC Couple, at the Club. This was in the 80's during the time of Sugar Bear's hit song "Doin the Butt", was popular. Occasionally K would jump on the stage with the DJ and start dancing; oh, we sure had some good ole times, and we would still get up on Sunday mornings to make it to church. For the most part, things were going well, and I thought we were growing as a family, but K was having issues with his work, so he expressed an interest in getting out of the military for medical reasons.

So, here I am, taking inventory. I am now thirty-eight weeks pregnant, and I'm now at the point where I am constantly tired, so when I went to my appointment, I asked the doctor what he could do to speed up the process to delivery. After his preliminary examination, and in response to my concerns, my doctor ruptured the sack causing my water to break the very next morning, which was two weeks before my due date. I called K to come home from work because it was time to go to the hospital. K was panicky and nervous because this was his first experience being a father. I had been through this twice already. But this time would not be as easy as my other two deliveries, because of some developed complications. I developed high blood pressure and the numbers were off the charts and the baby's heart rate was low, so this delivery was painful and uncomfortable. I had a blood pressure cup on the left arm, to monitor my pressure every twenty minutes, an IV on the right arm for fluids, and a tube running from the inside of me to monitor the baby's heart rate, so when a contraction occurred, I could not move to either my left or right side; all I could do was breathe and push down (as if I was using the bathroom) to relieve the pain. K is looking at me like he wanted, like he needed to do something to help me, but there was nothing he could do, so he leaves out, saying he needed to step out for a moment to get some fresh air, and that he was going to go home to get my Bible. How crazy was that! As I think back, it is quite hilarious now. By the time he returned to the hospital with my Bible, I had already delivered a healthy baby boy, so now, of course, K was a proud father. Our son was born in March and K had the whole house lit up with Christmas lights for the first week so that all the neighbors would know that we had the baby.

Upon my release from the hospital, I began to go through post-partum depression. I remember on the day leaving the hospital, after being discharged, K had the baby in his arms; I noticed that he was not showing me any warmth or affection, after delivering his child; he was not thinking of my wellbeing. He was not paying any attention to me –which was hurtful. He did not even open the car door for me to get in. He was so into the baby, he forgot, or so it seemed to me, that I did not exist at all in his eyes. I got in the car and then I burst out crying. I said, "*I just had your baby and you do not care about me!*" He laughed and raised my hand up like I was a champion and said, "You did it!" I ended up laughing myself. He had a way of making me laugh which made me forget about being upset with him. K was dedicated to getting up in the middle of the night, feeding, and taking care of the baby, and he did so for the first two weeks. However, when he returned to work after his family leave, he lost quite a bit of sleep, which began to wear him down, physically.

Even before the baby was born, our relationship started going downhill. I noticed that he would start arguments just to leave the house, and every time, I would fall for his trap, but then I would argue with him, and I would be glad when he rolled out. I remember one unfortunate Friday night after our son was born, he pointed his finger at my forehead and pushed my head back, called me fat, old and then, he had the audacity to say, *"You have three children; no one is going to want you,"* and walked out of the house. His words were cruel and mean and they tore me down to the core of my heart. I am sure many will agree that when a woman has a baby, she already does not feel attractive, and for him to speak to me in that manner really hurt me. Now, because of how things were going in our marriage, I started missing home and my family back in Washington DC. But, as God would intervene, He allowed me to meet a couple I had met there in Texas, who were from Washington DC; I do not know what I would have done if they had not come into my life. They were very supportive of our family. I also reconnected with my faith; this is the time I began watching Christian television in the mornings and this wonderful habit has followed me to this day.

Eventually, I started having consistent health challenges with high blood pressure, anxiety, and stress concerns so, consequently, a few weeks later I was riffed from my job; I was glad about this because I was now eligible for unemployment. I needed to rest and get my health in order. In the meantime, K was trying to get out of the military on disability. He had gotten very sick due to a tick bite while in the field. He started the conversations about our returning to Washington, DC so he started preparing me to get ready to go back, however, I did not want to return to the Washington DC area. I tried to convince him to stay in the military, but he was not having it. Then finally, one evening we were watching television and he turned the television off and stated that he needed to have a heart-to-heart talk with me. He explained that he did not want to be in the military, nor did he want to be married anymore. I asked what I could do to make things better or what could I do for him to help our marriage –for him to stay married to me, and, for a long while he said nothing. After a few minutes had passed, his reply was "*It is not you; it is me.*" He stated that he did not want the responsibility of taking care of three children. He did not want to be tied down in marriage and he wanted a new start. The conversation was not an argument, in fact, he was speaking from an honest place. So, after a few days had gone by, I decided to go see his Staff Sergeant. I asked him to help me persuade K to stay in the military and to stay in the marriage with me. His Sergeant said, "*Ma'am, he has made up his mind about a medical discharge, and about your marriage. I can't make him love you.*" I tell you; those words were like both a punch in my stomach and a slap in my face all at the same time.

It woke me up because I realized that I sounded pathetic; those words were a wake-up call. I had to tell myself, "*Girl, you have got to get it together! This man does not want you.*" And within a couple of months later, he received his military discharged papers. The military packed us up and K purchased airline tickets for me and the kids to return to Washington DC and that was the end of our marriage. Our son was only three months old when we returned to DC.

LESSON LEARNED:

When a man says: "He does not want to be with you anymore" and he says it in a calm and sincere manner (not angry), and he sets you down to break the news to you ever so gently, he means what he is saying, so save yourself from additional pain and agony.

You cannot make a person love you if they do not want to. Let them walk away to save your heart and seek God's peace. If you haven't already done so, quickly turn to Jesus, because He is the only one who loves us for all eternity and unconditionally.

So, we return to DC, and I only have eight hundred dollars in my bank account, three small kids, jobless and homeless for the first time in my life. K delivered my car to me a week or so after I arrived back home. He gave me the keys, and he quietly walked away; we did not speak for several months later until I contacted him when my money ran out. Here is the kicker! He did not want to have anything to do with his newborn baby—his only son. He was now back in the Washington DC area, living his best life. It appeared that he did not want to help me financially (on his own) which was disappointing, so I called him up one day to ask for money to buy pampers and milk for the baby and he said, "Ask your parents because I need to get some new tires for my car" and he hung the phone up on me. I was hurt, angry –I was bewildered; I couldn't believe what I had just heard, and I thought to myself, *Okay tires come before your son. We will see about that!* I had forgotten that before leaving El Paso, TX, K purchased a new beautiful white Audi, but he never told the dealership that he was getting out of the military and relocating to another state, so he forgot that I knew he had left El Paso, TX without providing a forwarding address to the dealership, and that he skipped town without letting them know anything. So, guess what I did – yep, you guessed right! I called the dealership and asked if they knew he had relocated to another state and the dealer replied, *"No! In fact, we have been looking for him for a few months, because he had not made a car payment."* Once he had the car over state lines, without an address, it was my belief that he had planned not to pay for the car. He had not paid the car note in ninety days and the dealership was looking for the car to repo it. The salesperson said, that if I gave them an address, and they picked up the car, that he would send me a check for $100. I did not know where K lived, but I did know where he worked, and I gave them the information. They went to his job site and picked up the car on a Friday. I wished I was there to see the expression on his face when he got off work and his car was gone. This is called, "Hurt people, hurt people". The car dealership mailed me that check and I went out and purchased pampers and milk for my baby, so K would not have to worry about pampers, milk or tires! That was the most vindictive thing I had ever done, and I must tell you, it felt great. Now I felt as if I was *not* the only one in this relationship dealing with the consequences of unwise choices made.

After that situation, we finally went to court for child support, and I started the paperwork to file for a divorce. It seemed as if it was not a big problem for him because he got another car shortly thereafter.

I found out that he met a new lady friend, and they started hanging out together and he started selling drugs to make extra money. This was alarming to me because K was not brought up in that type of environment; he was not even built for that type of life. He never smoked, drank, or used drugs while in the military. I do not know what was happening to him when he returned to the Nation's Capital; he just didn't appear to be the person I once knew. Subsequently, not too long after he purchased his new car, he was arrested. Since he was a first-time offender and recently discharged from the military he did not go to prison. I guess the judge had mercy on him. I had heard that he was assigned to a work-release program and that he was able to keep his job. He was now living in a halfway house, and while he was there is when I filed for the divorce. And that was the end for us. By the time he came to visit his son for his once and only time, I was already remarried. When he saw my wedding pictures, he saw that someone did want me, even with three children. And when he saw how happy we were, he decided to never come around again. I never kept my children from spending time with their fathers, it was the fathers' unwise choices to be absent from their child's life. K attended our son's graduation ceremony from high school, and that was because I reached out to him. However, he did not attend our son's wedding; he was invited but he did not show up. But that's between him and God. When our son turned twenty-three years old, he got into a motorcycle accident, and suffered a traumatic brain injury; he was in a deep coma, on a ventilator to keep him alive. The surgeon had to perform a craniectomy, to remove a part of his skull in order to relieve pressure from his brain. Our son was unrecognizable, and based on his condition, the medical staff stated that he was not going to survive. But our family stood on the Word of God; we were all in agreement and we declared like King David, that he shall live, and not die, and declare the works of the Lord. Bishop G prayed for him, our family, and when Bishop G sent this scripture, **Psalm 118:17** *"I shall not die, but live, And declare the works of the Lord"* via text, and this scripture became the foundation for our son's recovery.

One day, we were in a meeting with the neurologist, and he showed us a normal brain, and then showed us our son's brain, and nothing was there but blackness from all the bleeding on the brain. They suggested that we unplug the ventilator and let him die, but we all agreed and told them not to unplug the ventilator, that we were believing for a miracle. I asked if they were going to do everything medically to sustain my son's life and the doctor said, yes, but the way things were looking, if he lived, he would be in a vegetative state. Therefore, I reached out to my son's grandparents (K's father and stepmother). I did not have anyone's contact information on K's side of the family, even while going through this situation, I had to drive them to their home to inform them of what had happened. K's parents reached him, and they all came up to the hospital the very next day. I was not at the hospital when they arrived, but rather my husband was still with my son in the room. After K received the doctors' reports, he assumed that we were going to unplug the ventilator. My husband immediately called me to inform me that they were there, and my husband asked if I wanted to talk to my ex-husband; I said *Yes, put him on the phone.* When he got on the phone, the first thing he said, was, *when are you going to have them pull the plug?* Those words that came forth out of his mouth made me sick to my stomach, I was on my way back to the hospital, but I got so sick, I had to stop at a restaurant to use the bathroom; I regurgitated and had diarrhea all at the same time. I had never felt that sick in my entire life. I thought for a moment that I was going to die. After composing myself — after getting myself together I was back on the phone with K, and when he asked that question again, I immediately replied, that we absolutely have no intention in pulling the plug and I recited Psalms 118:17, and then I told K that we only wanted and needed people around us who were in alignment with us; that our son would live and not die. We wanted no negative discussions coming or going forth. K stated that he was only going by what the doctors had reported to him. But I asked myself, what should I have expected from a deadbeat dad anyway who never made any contributions to rearing or taking care of his son; he never had any emotional attachment or connection with his son, and he was only in the child's life for three months. So, I had to ask myself, why would he even agree that our son would live. He did not even know him. The only connection between the two of them was a court-ordered bi-weekly child support payment of $125. That was not even enough to pay for childcare. In addition, he had his family thinking that I was taking him to the cleaners for child support. It's not like he couldn't afford to take care of his child because he had a very good salary, and he could afford it, but he would rather spend all his money on himself. Also, he lied on me to his family, saying, I would not allow him to visit his son when all the while it was his lack of taking responsibility as a father and man. So yes, the woman who approached me in front of my apartment, with the red flag information about him being irresponsible, was correct about him!

Matthew 5:11 *"You are happy when people act and talk in a bad way to you and make it very hard for you and tell bad things and lies about you because you trust in Me." (NLV)*

It is important for me to make note that I forgave K a long time ago, even before our son's accident. I forgave him for myself, for my son, for my peace and for my blessings. The word bless means "happy", and I am so blessed. My son is blessed! Although he is still recovering, he is healed, no matter what the doctors' reports say, and, furthermore, he is not in a vegetative state as they initially diagnosed, and he has no assistance with breathing machines, or tubes of any kind attached to him. He is alert and he communicates well. He enjoys eating good food, listening to music, and being with his family and friends. Hence, we do not have time for unforgiveness. God is too good, and He is so merciful! If God can forgive me of my sins, then I choose to forgive others. And, just as there are consequences for unwise choices, there are bountiful blessings from making wise choices. I choose life. I choose God's way, so that both me and my son may live!

Deuteronomy 30:19 *"I call heaven and earth to record this day against you, that I have set before you life and death, blessing and cursing: therefore choose life, that both thou and thy seed may live:"* AMEN

CHAPTER 5

*"A man who has friends must himself be friendly, But there is a friend who sticks closer than a brother." **Proverbs 18:24***

PART ONE: BEST FRIEND

Remember, Jesus is a friend who sticks with us closer than a brother. Jesus is our source in all things and there is not a friend like the lowly Jesus, no not one. Therefore, do not think your best friend is really your best friend.

Dez and I were best friends; in fact, we go all the way back to high school, when we were trying to find ourselves and our place in the world. I call him my best friend because he stuck by my side and had my back during the most challenging times in my life. When we were in high school, he knew about my long-term relationship with Jay, since junior high school. All the other guys in our neighborhood knew not to look my way, because they were afraid of Jay. Dez was not afraid or intimidated by Jay's reputation. In fact, he wanted me to break up with Jay and become his girlfriend, but I refused to break up

109

with Jay. I was so attached to Jay I felt as if he was the man I was supposed to marry. But you know, my best friend Dez was very patient with me. I believe he was waiting for the right opportunity to move into Jay's spot. But that was never going to happen, and as time passed, he realized I was not going to leave Jay, so we remained best friends. Our relationship in the Greek term "Phileo love", is an emotional connection that goes beyond acquaintances or casual friendship, but it is not based on sexual connection, but rather a deeper level of connection (like having a BFF) but it's a guy. We shared our dreams, concerns, and problems, but Dez, being of the opposite sex, made our relationship more special and personal because we were attracted to each other. I could call him anytime, and he would be there for me. Dez kept a job, he had a car in high school – and he was a smooth talker, a classy gentleman and he made me feel exceptionally joyful when I was feeling down or sad about my relationship with Jay. But Dez was far from perfect. When we were in high school, he had a daughter, but he was not in a relationship with the mother; their hook-up was more like a one-night stand situation. Anyway, he loved his daughter with all his heart. And we bonded so much together by sharing our complicated situations; we had a lot in common. We would talk on the phone for endless hours. I remember his mother picking up the phone several times, telling him to get off the phone because she needed to use it. And he would say *okay Mom*, but he would stay on the phone until she picked the receiver up again. I would often tell him that we must get off the phone because his mother is not going to like me. I did not want his mother to think I was being disrespectful or disobedient to her. It was her son who refused to get off the phone with me, I guess he would say, it was the both of us!

I remember on our first date, he promised to make lunch for me. I was flattered because a guy never cooked for me before. He prepared fried chicken and boxed mac and cheese, and he set the table real nice with the plates and all, but when I bit into the chicken, the chicken was raw on the inside, with blood oozing. It was horrible. We had a good time laughing at his so-called cooking. He was the type of guy that a mother would like for her daughter, in fact, my mom always liked and approved of him. But we could never get together as a couple, we just remained the best of friends.

Even when I was pregnant with Jay's child, I would call Dez if I needed a ride to school and he would come and go out of his way, over to my side of town, and pick me up. I did complete my senior year and my child was born during the summer. And even after my child was born, Dez would stop by to visit us, always bearing gifts.

Now, at the time Dez and I are still special friends, he was dating a young lady who would later become his wife, even then, no one could break up our special friendship. A few months, after graduating, Dez joined the military and they got married, and unfortunately, we lost contact for several years. I had heard, during that time, that he was stationed in Germany. The next time I saw him, I was working at the Pentagon, and I ran into him in the halls of the Pentagon. BAM! I was single at the time! So, when I ran into him, I was very happy and excited to see him. The very next day we met for lunch to catch up on what we had been doing during for all those years apart. He stated that he and his wife were separated and planned to divorce. I thought to myself, finally, we can take our friendship to another level, and perhaps, we can get married? I was vulnerable and the excitement about the possibility of us getting together caused me not to question the circumstances of the divorce. In the past we were always open and honest with one another about our situationships, so I totally trusted him, I trusted his word. As the weeks went by, our lunches turned into dinners, and eventually, he visited me at my home. Things were going quite well between us, and my children liked him. After he "wined and dined" me, he drops the bomb on me telling me that his wife was pregnant, and that was the reason he had the temporary assignment at the Pentagon. He explained that they had gotten together while they were separated, and she ended up getting pregnant, during their separation. He explained that they just couldn't seem to work out their marital problems, but he insisted on sharing with me, that they were still going to get a divorce, and because he was in a similar situation when we were in high school, again, I believed him. He was truthful then about his situation, so why not believe him now? So, at lunch one Friday, we made plans to go out on a date that weekend. On that Saturday he did not show up or call. I called him, but he never picked up. He finally called me on that Monday and stated that the baby was delivered over the weekend, which was why he could not make it. That was a red flag for me because he could have still called to let me know what was going on. He told me that he would be around a few more weeks to help his wife with the baby and then he would return to Germany to finish his tour. But before he left, we got together, and he asked me to give him some time to take care of his family business. I promised that I would wait on him to get his personal affairs in order, so that we could finally, officially be together. His best friend and I drove him to the airport, we kissed and said goodbye.

That goodbye and our kiss –they were both, a real goodbye, because within a few months he writes me a Dear John letter, stating that he and his wife were reconciling and that she and the baby were there in Germany with him. He gave his wife my phone number, and she calls to verify that I got the letter. I told her I got the letter and yes, I receive the message loud and clear. I apologized to her and explained my side of the situation, that I was informed that they were not together and that they were getting divorced. She shared that yes, they were having marital problems, but that they never separated because he was the one who wanted to work things out. (STOP right here, ladies! Know this one thing: men will tell you whatever they think you want to hear to get what they want.) That was shocking and disappointing to me because I thought we were best friends. But he played me. She knew we were friends from high school before they got married, but she did not know the extent of our relationship, but when she found out (and I never knew how she found out, which really doesn't matter), I promised her that she will not have any problems with me trying to contact her husband again. I recovered quickly from that situation. I felt perhaps I deserved it; you know the old saying, "what goes around, comes around" and you reap what you sow. When we were in high school, he wanted to be more than best friends and he was patient with me when I would not break up with Jay, so I could not be angry about his situation. I had no hard feelings toward him; it was just not meant to be. I forgave him for his deception, and I returned the understanding and grace that he had always extended to me.

PART TWO: BEST FRIEND

Unbelievable, but yes, you guessed it — Dez would come back into my life one more time. He returns to

Washington DC, alone, because they could not work out their marital problems. His wife and their daughter moved to another state with her family. So, by the time we reconnect, I was a little more spiritual. I had received the infilling of the Holy Spirit with the evidence of speaking in tongues. My children and I were involved in various ministries. I was moving up in my professional career. My life was peaceful, and I did not want any drama or similar dramas to what had happened before. He would have to prove himself this time. I trust a person up to an extent until they are found untrustworthy. Once they break my trust, they must earn it and it will not be easy because I am going to question everything they do or say to me, and they would certainly be held accountable to me, for them to regain my trust. And that was not going to be easy for Dez! He was working in the area I had just moved back to, and a mutual friend of ours told him I was back and where I had moved. So, one day, he stopped by and knocks on my door. And just like that, we reconnected, as if nothing had ever happened between us. He jumps right in and starts helping me out with my children. I was traveling a lot for my job at the time, and when I had to go out of town, I did not have to inconvenience or interrupt my children's schedules because he would stay at my house and take care of them. He drove them to school, cooked dinner for them after school, helped with homework and he was showing me that he was ready to be fully committed to me. And I was thankful for his assistance. However, it seemed to me that he was taking his own sweet time in getting his divorce. I was not comfortable with the situation, and I felt convicted in my spirit as to our dating again. I made a quality decision that Dez had to get it together quickly and in a hurry if he wanted this new woman of God. But one weekend he went out of town to visit his daughter and I did not hear from him the entire time: another red flag and here we go again. So, when he returned and he came over to visit me, I broke off our growing relationship. What we are not going to do is play more games. We were getting too old for games. So, I told him to take care of his personal business and not contact me until it was done. From that day forward, we never spoke. And that was the end of my best friend and me, and by the time he finally got the divorce, I had met and married my current husband. Dez ended up remarrying also, and now we all are acquaintances, through our mutual friend to this day, in which we all get together from time to time, with our spouses and we all get along like mature adults, "the past is behind, the future is in front". And because the past is now behind us, we understand that it was not meant to be for us to be together, but rather the memories of *best friends*!

LESSON LEARNED:

Never, ever, ever get involved with a married person, even

if they say they are separated from their spouse, unhappy in the marriage, or let me wait until my kids are out of school, or until the kids get older or I am only with her/him for the kids' sake, or my spouse is ill, or it's complicated or for financial reasons, and oh, please don't forget this one, they say "I love you".

Whatever the reason is, save yourself from the drama, the headaches, the heartaches, and the consequences of being undervalued, because you are more than someone's side piece. And most importantly, God frowns on adultery.

Exodus 20:14 *"You shall not commit adultery."*

And just in case you think, well that's the Old Testament – and it's under the law.

Matthew 5:27 *"You have heard that it was said to those of old, 'You shall not commit adultery."*

Adultery is a sin, and there are no excuses or passes when it comes to sin. Repent and flee from immorality.

1 Corinthians 6:18 *KJV "Flee fornication. Every sin that a man doeth is without the body, but he that committeth fornication sinneth against his own body."*

Adultery, fornication, and other sexual sins are not of God, and they offend Him. Unfortunately, if we are vulnerable and caught off guard, we can fall into the enemy's trap every time, but I am so grateful to have since matured in the Lord and I have been enlightened, to flee from sexual immorality. I love God for who He is in my life, and I no longer desire to offend a Holy God.

When I started studying and learning God's Word for myself, reading the Holy Scriptures, and understanding what I meant to God, God started working on my heart. I was being transformed, truly into His likeness. I was beginning to know who I was in Him, and just how much He loves me; this brought conviction. Therefore, when Dez tried to come back into my world with the same old mindset, that things were going to be like they were before, he was sadly mistaken, I was growing and maturing in grace, and I was not about to get caught up offending my God with my best friend, or for anyone, for that matter.

I believe everything happens for a reason because this "situationship" helped me to understand how people can get caught up in situations like the experiences I've had for years. I finally realized that I was wasting precious time when I could have been in a devoted relationship with someone who honored God and had respect for me. No judging on my part, because Lord knows I understand how folk can look down upon you. I have been there! I take this time to encourage anyone who is caught up in this type of situation herein to go before the Lord and repent from sin, (meaning make a U-turn) and get out of that situation.

Lastly and most importantly, Do Not Judge!

Matthew 7:1-5 *"Judge not, that you be not judged. For with what judgment you judge, you will be judged; and with the measure you use, it will be measured back to you. And why do you look at the speck in your brother's eye, but do not consider the plank in your own eye? Or how can you say to your brother, 'Let me remove the speck from your eye', and look, a plank is in your own eye? You Hypocrite! First, remove the plank from your own eye, and then you will see clearly to remove the speck from your brother's eye."*

Think about this...

Other people's sins are not your business, and your sins are not their business. It is between them, their conscious and God, because they are the only ones who must and will stand in the Judgment Seat of Christ!

And like Forrest Gump said, "That is all I gotta say about that!"

CHAPTER 6

"Love suffers long and is kind; love does not envy; love does not parade itself, is not puffed up; does not behave rudely, does not seek its own, is not provoked, thinks no evil; does not rejoice in iniquity, but rejoices in the truth; bears all things, believes all things, hopes all things, endures all things. Love never fails." 1 **Corinthians 13:4-8**

We would do well to study, meditate, and grow in understanding the meaning of this scripture. It is not an overnight process for us to operate and act on what the Apostle Paul wrote about concerning true love. It can take years of maturing in the things of God, but nonetheless, love never fails.

First, what is a Knight in Shining Armor? Who is he? He is an idealized or chivalrous man who comes to the rescue of a woman in a difficult situation. And that is who my beloved husband, of almost thirty years, is to me!

So let me share our journey with you.

We met through mutual friends. My husband was the guy's friend, and the wife was mine. Our marriage could compare to an episode of "Marriage at First Sight" (a television program where couples meet and marry their spouse at first sight at their wedding ceremony); our wedding was not at first sight, but it happened three months after our initial meeting. At least my husband and I were acquainted three months prior to our getting married. I definitely would not recommend anyone to do that, because you do not know much about the person you are about to make a covenant to God with, and marriage, it's serious business! My first impression of my husband was that he was a very nice individual, humble and unpretentious. I had not seen him in person; we spoke over the phone a couple of weeks prior to our meeting face to face. My friend gave him my phone number and told him to give me a call, in hopes that we would all go out on a double date. But seemly, every time we planned to get together, something would come up, and the scheduled dates had to be postponed. Therefore, we had spoken enough that I felt comfortable inviting him over to my home for dinner without chaperones. When he rang my doorbell and I looked through the peephole and saw this beautiful man standing on the other side of the door, my heart dropped to my stomach. I thought to myself, oh my goodness. I must have won the lottery! He was tall, dark, attractive, and muscular. We had spoken over the phone for a couple of weeks, and I knew he was an extremely intelligent person. So, when I saw him, he appeared to be the whole package deal. That feeling of butterflies in my stomach came over me once again, and it took me back to when I was a young girl. I had not felt this way about anyone in years. I opened the door and he entered bearing gifts: he brought flowers and a perfume gift set. He was a gentleman, and I was very impressed. My children were home, so I called them downstairs to introduce him to them. And when my oldest son gave me a thumbs up, it made me feel good to have his approval. I invited him into the living room to have a seat; there we sat and talked for a while. Then my oldest child wanted to go to the skating rink with his friends, and I had to drive him there. It was during winter, cold, and dark outside, and I did not want to take my two other younger children out at the time, so I asked him if he wouldn't mind watching them until I return home from dropping my son off at the rink. I did not know if this man was a serial killer, a thief, a rapist, or even a crazy person. But I trusted my gut and the conversations we had over the two-week period, and it gave me enough confidence that he was a good person. So yes, I left my babies with a stranger. Trusting people without verifying their character has been one of my personal downfalls in life. I thank God for protecting me and my children in those gullible moments of my life. Well, nothing happened to them, and they kept him company and preoccupied while I made the twenty-minute drive. Upon returning home, we had a nice seafood dinner, and he enjoyed my cooking. I knew I had him when I fed him some shrimp. He smiled and stated that no woman had done anything nice like that for him in a very long time. From that night forward, we were inseparable.

I need to inject here, that before we met, I was settled and content with being alone. I had broken up with Dez and told him not to come back to me until he was divorced, so I was not looking for a relationship at all. I was active in my church and at peace with myself. Please note, that I am not saying I had it all together just because I was consistently going to church, and this does not mean that my mind was renewed because renewing your mind is a process, as it takes time in prayer, studying God's Word and setting under anointed teachers and preachers in the church. As I mentioned earlier, my older children were involved in ministry; they were a part of the Baptist Conference, traveling with the church to conventions. We were comfortable and I was financially stable enough that I did not need a man to financially provide for us; I was providing for our basic needs, and a few wants. I was moving up in my career as a financial manager and I was also growing in ministry; teaching Sunday School, attending Bible Study, and regular church services, consistently and fervently. Also, my church sent me to an amazing, enlightening, anointed retreat center that changed my life forever, called "A Walk to Emmaus". The

Emmaus Retreat challenged me to find the role Jesus played in my life, spending quality time in quiet prayer and my reflecting on the love of Jesus; it was like I had a sweet, precious visitation with Jesus–just like the two disciples who were walking along the road from Jerusalem to Emmaus, in the Bible story in Luke 24:13-35. I had truly learned some life-changing teachings from that Retreat, and after that experience, I wanted to serve God even the more. I desired to be a better woman of God and in renewing my mind to walk in victory. I wanted to make better choices. I had chosen to seek first the Kingdom of God and His righteousness, which is God's way of living, being, and doing.

Matthew 6:33 *"But seek first the kingdom of God and His righteousness, and all these things shall be added to you."*

Surely, God would provide a godly man for me. And, by the time I met my husband, I had already acquired a dedicated and committed relationship with the Lord. Fortunately, my husband had come into my life when I was in a good place, spiritually. I invited him to church, then to dinner to meet my parents. We shared our goals, hopes, and dreams for the future. He explained that he wanted a committed relationship to keep himself focused and on the right track, as he had made unwise choices and, he too, experienced the consequences which resulted in him being away for a while, but long enough for him to obtain two degrees, so with that, he expressed that he was looking forward to getting married and having children. I explained my concern to him that with my having three children with three different fathers, and, although I love my children with all my heart and soul, I had no plans to have another child with a fourth father who could or would possibly leave us fending for ourselves. I had been there and done that enough in my lifetime. As the quote by Albert Einstein says: "Insanity is doing the same thing over and over again and expecting different results." That was, finally, a revelation to me. I had enough of people looking down on me, especially the church. I made that choice before we met, I took matters into my own hands, and I stood by my decision. But isn't it something how life will throw you a curveball! Just when I was at peace, content being single and raising my three children alone, and not looking for love or a husband, here comes this beautiful opportunity my way. So, I thought, since we both knew what we wanted going forward, why wait? I was involved in the church, and I did not want to get into a fornication stronghold situation again. Therefore, I shared my faith, I initiated the topic of marriage and we decided to get married.

1 Corinthians 7:2 *"Nevertheless, because of sexual immorality, let each man have his own wife, and let each woman have her own husband."*

You must be sure that you heard from God if you decide to marry a person in such a brief time of knowing them. Our marriage was an experiment. We did not know each other, nor did we love one another like Christ loved the church and gave Himself for it.

Ephesians 5:25-26 *"Husbands, love your wives, just as Christ also loved the church and gave Himself for her, that He might sanctify and cleanse her with the washing of water by the word,"*

Neither one of us knew anything about Christ and the church. We would learn that years later in our marriage. That is why marriage counseling is so especially important. In our two marriages, neither of us had pre-marital counseling. My first marriage was based on personal motives, and we were only together for two years and divorced by the third year. In our current marriage, we did not have pre-marital counseling either, so I encourage all couples to get pre-marital counseling to ensure they have a clear understanding of what they are getting into, from every aspect of life, which will involve spiritual, physical, financial, communicative, honesty, and trust. We had one such meeting with my pastor and he asked a few questions like — did my husband have a job, does he accept my children, and what date did we want to get married? And that was it, we all know that there is more to marriage than those few questions. He did not mention anything about wives submitting to their own husbands, as unto the Lord, or husband love your wives like Christ loved the church, hence, we started off wrong. I was the head of my three children and household. I did not need anyone telling me what I needed to do. I was already running my household. I already knew what was good for my family. Honestly, it was a big adjustment for me to have to consult with another person. My husband was raised in a more traditional household, wherein his father was the head of their household, and his mother was more of the homemaker and submissive wife, (Momma T was doing the Word), however, a traditional household was a little different from what I was accustomed to.

Ephesians 5:22 (NKJV) "Wives, submit to your own husbands, as to the Lord."

In the way I was raised, women were independent. They led their families; my mother worked two jobs, just as my father did, therefore I saw an equal partnership working together to achieve a common goal which was to provide a better life for us all. Note: Your family dynamics make a difference when you choose a spouse. This brings me back to the point I stated earlier in this chapter, to get to know a person before marriage.

Within a few weeks of our marriage, we got into a big argument because I decided to do something without consulting him. He was saying if I am going to make my own decisions. I do not need him, and he threatened to leave. So, throughout the years, it has been a process of learning several key components of a good marriage, how to submit, include, and consult my husband before making decisions on my own. As well as I had to learn to trust his style of parental guidance. *Oh boy*, did I have a hard time releasing my babies into his total care as *daddy*, and after a while, this discouraged him to the point wherein he said that he felt he could not fulfill his role as a dad. This was due to my running interference whenever he disciplined the children. This caused disagreements because his way of discipline was not the way I thought he should discipline them. These were just some of his concerns which made him feel like he was not needed as a husband or dad. These were some of the issues that brought division between us. He became frustrated and disconnected from me, which was the beginning of him making unwise choices that allowed the devil to come in and wreak havoc in our marriage. So, when you get married and have a blended family, you must trust that your spouse has the best interests of the family at heart. I had a hard time adjusting to having a man who took his role in parenting so seriously as my husband did. Situations like this can cause a major breakdown in marriage.

Also, when we met, my husband shared that he was

seeking a woman with spiritual values as he desired to prosper and live a successful life. We knew spirituality would help during difficult times. We both had to learn how to be patient with each other. He would tell me that I am all he has and that it is important that I believe in him. Honestly, I did not understand *that* at the time. I was thinking, he has a father, a mother, and siblings so please tell me, how is it that I am all he has? But what he was really saying (and meaning) was that we are now one —one with each other. *He would say things like "It is just you and me to conquer the world."* He was older and wiser regarding the husband's role in leading the family, but I had been leading my children since I was eighteen years old, therefore, this transition and the adjusting was difficult for me. Even with spiritual insight, marriage is an adjustment. We had morning prayer, watched Christian television, and listened to Christian radio and music. During those days, we had one car in the mornings, taking the children to school, we would have them recite scripture, and we would pray and sing Christian songs, and my oldest son would make beats hitting his books or the back of the seat as we sang. My husband had practiced Islam and had studied many other religions. He once stated that there are many ways to God. But as time went on and we joined a non-denominational Church, he learned that Jesus is the only way to God.

John 14:6 *"Jesus said to him, "I am the way, the truth, and the life. No one comes to the Father except through Me."*

The spiritual foundation in our marriage was the fundamental reason we made it through the storms in our marriage and in life.

Like I said earlier, we did not have marriage counseling when we got married. The pastor asked if he had a job, well yes, he had a job, but it was not going to provide the lifestyle we had discussed when sharing our goals. He was working with a youth program, which was great for the children. In this position, he got them involved with various athletic activities. This job caused my children to bond with him alone. He became daddy! He then enrolled in a medical training program, to become a paramedic or Emergency Room (ER) technician. Once he completed training and graduated, he landed a position in the ER. But he was not there very long because one of his responsibilities was to take deceased bodies to the hospital morgue. One day, he met this lady who worked for an organ donor organization. During one of their many conversations, she inquired about his qualifications to do that job. I am not sure how everything went down, but she ended up introducing him to the director of the company. He went through the training process and obtained a great job becoming a technician extracting eye tissue and organs, for research and transplant. And in no time, he became the office manager. This position allowed him flexibility; he was out of the office most of the time going to different hospitals promoting organ donations. He had to wear a pager because he would be on call in the evenings and weekends. Things were looking up for our family. We were unified and we were achieving our goals. God blessed us with blessings upon blessings, along with a new home, so we moved to Maryland. We had new cars, credit cards, going on dates, taking trips, and job promotions and he moved up faster than I did in such a short timeframe. In the early stages of our marriage, he was my ideal husband. My knight in shining armor and he took a lot of pressure off me as a single parent. I did not know how stressed out I had become, until I started having anxiety attacks. He helped me navigate through that process so that I would not have to take medications to calm down. I had just become overwhelmed with running around all the time; running many errands because we still lived in Washington, DC. I took the children to Maryland for childcare and school, then I drove from Maryland to Virginia to work. Also, I believe the prior traumatic "situationships" had taken an effect on my mental and emotional well-being. I had been through a lot, and now I have support and I could now relax. I began to learn more about the anxiety and stress and what the triggers were for me and what supplements would help lessen the attacks, along with deep breathing exercises, prayer, and meditation. And after a time, by

God's amazing grace, and the love and support of my husband, I overcame the anxiety and the stress attacks. I am healed.

There were a lot of positive things that happened in our marriage before the adversities and negative situations begun. When God started blessing us, the devil started messing with us. I really felt like that is what started happening. My husband had a promising career; financially we were in a good place and on the outside looking in, we had the appearance of a good marriage, however, we were not doing the work to maintain a *godly* marriage. Getting to the place where we understood God's principles in marriage would be a work in progress.

I noticed a change in my husband; he no longer was accountable to me as being his wife, his helpmate. He was not communicating his whereabouts, not checking in, and when I confronted him, he would say, he was working, which was not always the truth. When I paged him, he would not respond for hours, and he would wait until he was on his way home hours later to call, or he would not call at all. I started becoming suspicious because he started acting differently toward me. He would keep his cell phone with him all the time; this was a red flag, and he would become very secretive. So, I started checking up on him when he told me he was working. I would follow up with a call to the "donor call center" and they would tell me if he was on call or not. My calls were so frequent that the operators became familiar with me, and one operator asked, why is your husband lying about being at work? I said, *apparently, he is using his job as an excuse to be out after his work hours were over.* The operator must have felt sorry for me because she told me to call anytime, and she would let me know his schedule. And that is how I developed an inside connection. He hated that. He tried to manipulate me by saying, he is going to lose his job if I keep on calling the "call center line" but I had made inside connections and if he had nothing to hide, it should not be a problem for a wife to call her husband's job. One thing I was not going to do was turn my head and ignore the signs of cheating. I became my own detective, and I did my own homework. We both worked about 30 minutes away from each other at that time, and I usually would get off work before he did, so a few times after work, I would drive to his building and wait until he got off work and I would follow him. One time he came straight home, one time he went to the mall, and finally one time to a townhouse development down the street from his job. I watched him go into this townhouse, and of course I am unfamiliar with this resident –the person he was about to visit. I did not know if it was work-related by it being so close to his office building, so I waited for some time before I approached him about this visitation. I needed a little more information and proof. I wrote down the address to see if

I could get the name of the resident. Information was not as readily available online like it is today. So, it took me a while to find out who was the resident of that townhome. You see, this phase in our marriage was called, *sleeping with the enemy*. I started going through his coats and jackets and one day I found a picture. And that is when I confronted him. I told him the address and that I saw him go into the townhouse. He took the photo from me, and he burned it. Then he confessed to me who the person (the woman) was. He tried to blame me for his infidelity, trying to turn the situation around to make me believe or feel like it was all my fault. His reasoning to me was that I did not pay enough attention to him, and we were drifting apart. He tried to become a master at manipulating me. But I was not having it, I was not going to allow him to blame me for his infidelity. I was totally dependent on God and spirituality (walking with God and doing things the best I knew to do as a Christian wife) when our marriage became difficult; I did not cheat on my husband. Therefore, I can give no blame on infidelity!

Doing this process, I had to learn how to put my faith in God to handle the situations. So, when I found out that he was cheating on me, I was very hurt, disappointed in him, and angry. We had supported each other for years, up until this point. We had grown together in reaching our goals and receiving many blessings from God. Yes, I was extremely hurt and angry and I slapped him in his face, and I demanded an explanation. I cried and cried; it was bad. He just sat on the edge of the bed, hung his head down like a child being scolded, and took my scolding and rebuke.

At the beginning of our marriage, I really and truly trusted him with my whole heart regarding being faithful. I honestly believed; *"That my knight in shining armor had finally come to my rescue."* I believed that I had finally found a loyal partner to spend the rest of my life with. Although we had issues in the adjusting phase, I was not expecting this to happen to me again. And as I had mentioned in the previous chapter about trust, I have always given my trust to people upfront, be it males, females, family, friends, in ministry, at work until it is broken, and once it is broken it takes a long time –perhaps years to regain my trust. Trust would have to be earned going forward. I am like a child in that respect. I generally trust people and believe in the good of all mankind, until I am violated in some way.

Anyway, my husband apologized and promised to break it off. He stated we could start over again. But it was hard for me to believe in him because the trust was broken, and I did not know how deep he was involved in the relationship with this *other woman.* Again, this was our second marriage for the both of us, and I did not want it to end in divorce. I really wanted it to work. I had grown to know and love my husband during our years together;

yes, he is a bit complicated, and I believed he just wanted to do his own thing. Well, as I thought and considered, I discovered that he did not break off the relationship immediately. Instead, he tried to be more accountable to me by calling me more, but he was still seeing her. Out of frustration and lack of control over the situation I went to his job parking lot and took the car he was driving. I had one of my colleagues to ride with me to where the car was located and I took his car, and she drove my car to her home. He had never met her, so he did not know where to find the car. I left that car in her yard for several days, just to prove a point to him that I am in control of the situation. So, I thought I was sending a message to him that he could lose everything he had. I wanted to remind him that what is his, is mine as well. We built these things, this life together. I was just reaching for stars to get his attention. Of course, he was furious when he went to that parking space and the car was gone. That move made the situation worse because he was angry now because he needed his car to do his job. But you know what, I got his attention at that very moment! To prevent him from taking the car I was driving, I put one of those security jacks on my steering wheel. He had to rent a car until I finally gave the car back to him. I was hurting and I felt betrayed so I thought I would show him how it felt to be betrayed by someone you thought loves you.

As I mentioned earlier, "Hurt people, hurt people". That

is why it is imperative, to work on forgiveness and healing. When a person is hurt, they can potentially act out of character. And I knew that I fit that description. I was acting totally out of character. We ended up talking, and he asked if I wanted him to move out of our home. I said, "*Yes, I want you to move out.*" However, when I calmed down, I realized that I did not mean it. The next day when I had gone off to work, he packed his clothes, and without a hint, a note, call or nothing, he was gone. I came home from work, got undressed to start making dinner and when I opened the closet door and saw his side empty —all his clothes were gone, I was shocked. Once he moved out, I really, then, had second thoughts about telling him I wanted him to move out. But it was too late, he was gone, and it was a done deal.

LESSON LEARNED:

Say what you mean and mean what you say. Once words are out in the atmosphere, they cannot be taken back.

Matthew 5:37 *"But let your 'Yes' be 'Yes,' and your 'No,' 'No.' For whatever is more than these is from the evil one."*

I just got played and the enemy got me. I said yes, but I meant no, because I allowed pride and anger to get in the way of truth. And the truth was, I did not want to get divorced a second time in life. He wanted a way out anyway, and I gave him what he wanted very easily.

Therefore, he was able to shift the blame on me, by saying, that I told him to leave.

We separated for eight months. During that time, I had the woman's home number, and from time to time I called her house asking for him, but her English was not good, or she was acting like she did not understand English. You probably can relate to how some people may act like they don't know what is going on or what's really happening when they know very well, they are doing the wrong things, well yep, this was how she seemed to me. I had called her from my work phone, and I honestly don't remember what I said to her, but she said that I frightened her. I guess she thought this lady is crazy calling my house asking about her husband. She knew I took his car, so I guess she did not know what I would be capable of doing next. She was intimidated and ended up calling the police on me. I should have not even spoken to that poor woman. She was not my problem; my husband was my problem. I did not know her, and she did not know me. In the situation, I believe I did intimidate this poor woman; she had a police officer contact me. The officer identified himself with a badge number, and he told me that he had my work numbers and the voice messages I had left her. He also told me that I was using government property (my desk phone) and that I could lose my job if the woman pressed charges. He advised me not to contact her again or she will be pressing charges against me for harassment. Of course, I told the officer that I understood and that she will never have to worry about me contacting her again because I had too much to lose. That was the end of me ever looking her way, as well as my husband, because he did not appreciate her calling the police on me. Instantly whatever relationship they had was over, and my husband was back home.

LESSON LEARNED:

The other woman is not the problem.

The husband has the dilemma, the quandary, if you will, and he must figure out the right way to live, and the right way to treat his wife. He must be accountable to God first, then to his wife, and if a man does not have a relationship with God, he is basically doing his own thing, based on his life experiences, character, and/or upbringing. If a man has issues with infidelity, he must work out his demons and his soul salvation.

After all of this had taken place, a few weeks later, I thought that perhaps we both needed counseling, so eventually we both attended marriage counseling together and one of the first things the counselor stated specifically to him, of course, was that she could counsel us both, however, she will not counsel us and outside women. She suggested a book about a man's battle with infidelity. In our sessions, she also suggested that if someone else is involved, he needed to break off that relationship, if he wanted to honestly work on our marriage. My husband purchased the book, however, after that session, he never went back to a session with that therapist, and he did get the true understanding and information about infidelity, which proved to be very helpful to us in our marriage.

Hebrews 13:4 *"Marriage is honorable among all, and the bed undefiled, but fornicators and adulterers God will judge."*

My past actions and reactions were out of God's will, but when you know better, you do better. I had no business calling or checking for any women on behalf of my husband because my husband was my problem. I needed to deal with him and him alone. But back then, I allowed my emotions to get in the way which distorted my reasoning or thinking, and I was also making the other women my problem and the cause of my "situationship". The other woman and I did not have anything to do with each other, rather my husband had the dilemma. The other women are not the cause of infidelity; they are the effect (the result) of the man's issues of being unfaithful. An unwise choice we make is blaming the other woman. I have since learned that rather than blaming others outside of my marriage, I must focus on my marriage and seek positive ways to reconcile my/our differences.

When my husband moved out of our home, I do not

believe he planned on getting a divorce, or he would have filed for it right away. Because the entire time, he paid the bills, as usual, cut the grass, and continued the upkeep of the house. He attended the children's activities and church services as if we were living in the home together. He is a very private person, and he did not want anyone to know we were in an unfortunate place in our marriage. Most of his family members did not even know we were separated. The neighbors did not know for sure because they would see him coming and going. When he did move back in, I believe it was not noticeable; it was like nothing ever happened. So now, when I see a neighbor's car gone overnight or for days on end, (the car is out more than in), I have flashbacks to when we were in a bad place within our marriage.

You never know what is going on in a person's home or life unless they share it. We were looking like a united front and going to church every Sunday like a stabled functioning family, however, we were very dysfunctional. There are many families living in this type of dysfunction today –right in our churches – and needing support so that they too can have a healed successful marriage. But unfortunately, people are so concerned about what others are going to say or think about them. Like we did, they too pretend to have a successful marriage. They pretend they have the best children in the world, all while they are suffering and struggling in silence, trying to hold things together. The bottom line, people are not perfect, we all fall short of God's glory.

Proverbs 24:16 *"For a righteous man may fall seven times And rise again, But the wicked shall fall by calamity."*

And when we own that fact, we can get free from what people think or say about us; having a relationship with the Lord and a strong spiritual foundation is what causes our marriage to sustain during hardships, tests, and trials. Although we were going through trials in our marriage (and we were "faking it until we made it"), we never stopped going to church, watching Christian television and movies, or listening to Christian music. Being accountable in attending church was also helpful. Never run away from church when you are going through difficult times. Difficult times are the times when you need to hear the Word of God the most.

I personally never stopped studying God's Word or lessons in preparation to teach in Children's Church. This is what helped us. What you expose yourself to, you will eventually turn your heart toward it. We both had a responsibility to the ministries we supported, and we both continued working diligently in our ministries without skipping a beat. In our case, one of the ministries we supported and attended at the time of us going through was big on building families, and communities and involving the whole family unit in ministry, no matter what age, or status of the family. They encouraged families to grow up in and take God's principles to heart. They had mandatory marriage meetings wherein couples could come in and watch Jimmy Evans's marriage conference videos. Those videos were extremely helpful in providing tools to improve our marriage. I would have to say, it was the church connections that helped us understand what a successful marriage looked like. It was hearing the Word of Truth, having a spiritual foundation, accountability, and the willingness on both our parts to do the work during those difficult times. And when I confided in our Pastors about our situation, they were very intentional and instrumental in helping us with accountability. The senior Pastor reached out to my husband until they connected and for that, I will always be grateful. The Pastor became a point of accountability as a man of God. He did not make my husband feel bad about what was going on; he listened, then shared the good news of Jesus, what the Word states about marriage, and how a husband is supposed to love his wife.

He explained to my husband that if he does not treat his wife right, his prayers will be hindered. He shared that God gave a Word to husbands.

1 **Peter** 3:7 *"Husbands, likewise, dwell with them with understanding, giving honor to the wife, as to the weaker vessel,*

and as being heirs together of the grace of life, that your prayers may not be hindered."

And I had to understand that I had accountability to my husband as well.

1 Peter 3:1 *"Wives, likewise, be submissive to your own husbands, that even if some do not obey the word, they, without a word, may be won by the conduct of their wives."*

The Pastor broke the Word down for us so that we understood that we could bring the best out of our marriage by understanding and applying God's Word to our lives. We both learned to love each other like Christ loves the Church. Christ laid down his life for the Church, and when we honestly, truly "really" receive Christ as our Lord and Savior. He lives inside our hearts, and we do have the ability to live a holy life without blemish in the sight of the Lord. When we please our Lord, we will not be walking in darkness or doing our own thing.

Concerning the consequences for my husband, things started going wrong for him concerning his career and finances; the favor of God was not showing up as in the previous years. He began to realize, he had to make some changes in his life.

I am grateful that we survived that first situation with

the help of our church. But there would be more trials and tribulations in our marriage to overcome. And I will continue to share to help my readers and others, to realize that if we survived all these issues in our marriage with the Lord as our helper, you too could survive your trials and tribulations as well.

We made unwise choices with our finances; the mistakes we made resulted in $70,000 in debt, caused by an audit from the IRS. My husband did not let me know about the tax audit, but what does he do, he hides the letters from the IRS. Like Mister in "The Color Purple" movie. Mister hides Celie's letters from her sister who was in Africa with Celie's children. Well, my husband hid the IRS letters from me. I just happened to get the mail one day and saw a letter from the IRS. When I opened it, I said to myself, this must be a mistake. So, the next day, I called the IRS to inquire about it. The agent on the other end stated that they had been trying to contact me for almost a year. The agent said, are you setting down, then she begins to tell me how much we owed for audited results they prepared because we did not address the letters. So, by the time I addressed the situation, the bill was about seventy thousand dollars in payments, penalties, and interests, which is the cost of a small house in some parts of the country. Messing with my money was worse than adultery! I was very disappointed in him for keeping this from me, because in my position at the time, we had to report any financial situations like owing the IRS, or any debt we owe, we had to sign a waiver. They made us sign a waiver to prevent potential bribery for Government information. My job would have been on the line if I would not have found out in time enough to do something about the situation. It took some years, but we worked our way out of that situation by God's amazing grace and mercy. We have been through it all, financially, which caused more problems in the marriage. From that point, my husband promised to be transparent with me regarding our finances, or any business dealings with me.

Here is a Proverb about being dishonest:

Proverbs 11:1-3 *"Dishonest scales are an abomination to the Lord, But a just weight is His delight. When pride comes, then comes shame; But with the humble is wisdom. The integrity of the upright will guide them, But the perversity of the unfaithful will destroys them."*

My husband, I believe, began to realize that he could not continue being private –as he would say, and deceptive – as I would say, therefore, in God's timing, he humbled himself before God, but with me, we still had a long road ahead of us to get to the place we are today.

You see, we both knew how to push the other's buttons. Before we both grew up in the things of God we would argue, and I would get angry with him because he would antagonize me by saying mean words and laughing in my face during arguments or when I would catch him in a lie. I would physically hit and push him. I thought I could hit and push him around because I believed he would never hit a woman. Honey, but one day, on a Sunday and it was the fourth of July. My husband and I got into a domestic violence situation. We were all getting ready for church; he was in the shower, and I was getting dressed. I was looking for a blouse to wear with my suit. I went into the laundry room, but it was not hanging where I left it to dry. He moved my blouse placing it into a laundry basket with other clothes. I could not find the blouse; it was a dressy blouse, meaning if you put it in a laundry basket it would surely get wrinkled. In my continuous frustration about some other things (which had nothing to do with the blouse), I went into the bathroom and asked if he moved my clothing, and he said yes, because the clothes had been hanging in the laundry room for weeks, so he decided to move them. I started fussing with him, saying, leave my clothes alone. I respect your clothes so leave mine alone. He replied you leave your clothes hanging around for weeks, so I put them in a laundry basket. Of course, I did not like his answer. He had a couple of his robes hanging in the bathroom, so I took the robes and threw them into the shower, while he was showering, telling him again that I do not touch your stuff, so do not touch mine. This is how it feels when someone disrespects your stuff. I turned around and he was getting out of the shower, and as he stepped out, he balled up his fists and punched me in the face three times, right, left, right punch just like a professional boxer. His fist hit my teeth and put a hole next to my lip and you could see straight through to my teeth. The blood started pouring out all over the place. And when he saw what he did he froze, staring at me like he was in a daze. We both walked out of the bathroom, and I yelled out you hit me in my face, and when I said that our youngest son came running into the room. He ran toward my husband like he was going to fight him, but I stepped between them, grabbed my son, and pulled him back, saying no, no, no do not fight him. My husband never moved, he was in shock, he just stood there naked, with his hands still balled up in a fist, like he was ready to knock our son out next. I noticed a lot of blood running down my clothing. So, I walked away and said, you are going to jail today. I called 911; the police arrived at the house in minutes, and they saw how I could not stop the bleeding, and they arrested him on the spot. He went to jail that day, and the ambulance came and took me to the hospital. Now here I am again in a humiliating, devastating situation. A female detective comes to the hospital to take pictures of my face, and she encourages me to go to the police station after being seen by the doctor to take out a restraining order against my husband. Once he got out of jail, he could not come near me or the home. The next day when he was released, he had his brother come over to the house to get some of his clothing, and he immediately moved in with his parents. When we went to court, he apologized to me, and to the court for losing his temper. He told the judge that when I threw his clothes into the shower, he lost control for a second. To be honest, the domestic violence situation arrived from being frustrated in our marriage. I will admit that I was the physical abuser when I got upset and he was the mental abuser who would antagonize me with hurtful words. The blouse was the cause of the incident. I was feeling disrespected about other things going on in our marriage and that was the tipping point. In my mind, this was the final straw; it would be over between us now. But no...no...no he was remorseful about the whole situation. He went to my parents' home and apologized to them, to all my siblings saying this would never, ever happen again if I take him back. My boys were not having it. They did not want to even look at him. It would take them some time to regain their respect and trust in him, but they eventually came around, because our daughter advocated for my husband. She had seen me hit and push my husband several times, and he never put his hands on me, so she tells her brothers that mom has been hitting daddy whenever she was angry with him, and this was the first time he hit her, she advises them to forgive him. When we went to court my boys were right by my side, ready to protect me and they did not speak to him, nor would they allow him to come near me. After reading the police report and hearing my husband's apology to me and to the court for his behavior, the judge must have thought our situation was worth working on because he made it mandatory that we both go to counseling. We separated again and attended counseling sessions for several months and we worked on ourselves, individually as well as attending sessions together as a couple to work on the marriage. It was complex, but I realized we loved one another during the process. My husband got down on his knees and asked for my forgiveness. Of course, I forgave him.

From that point forward we both never raised our hands toward one another. A changed behavior is attainable. People say, once a man hit you, he will do it again, but that has not been our case. We both learned not to put our hands on each other, and we both learned to control our emotions. Also, the counseling did what it was intended to do by providing us with tools we could use together to manage conflict. Counseling was beneficial, as I learned a lot about myself during the exercises the counselor gave me. I learned the root cause of my anger issues stemmed from childhood, my being bullied, and being teased which affected my self-image. Also, being in all those toxic relationships, the years of betrayal, lack of respect, and not being validated by any of those "situationships" caused the hidden rage. Until now, I had never felt any man truly loved me, except my earthly father who always made me feel safe, appreciated, loved, and valued. I highly recommend counseling when there is internal conflict. There are people in the African American community who may disagree with me about counseling; some even frown on it, but counseling helped me to pause, take a breather, and talk about my traumatic life experiences. The counseling helped to relieve stress and helped me resolve the traumatic experiences and regard them as "Lessons Learned" (LL) which allowed me to have greater self-confidence, regaining emotional balance and tools to have better relationships period. Now I have learned to set boundaries with toxic people, and I truly love them from a genuine place in my heart. Christian counseling is even more beneficial. I have attended both types of counseling. We learned a lot about ourselves, which was helpful. And once we started working together, we were able to reconcile our differences, in time. Things got better between us. Then things got worse, then finally things got better.

"Faith is taking the first step even when you don't see the whole staircase."

Dr. Martin Luther King, Jr.

Dr. King used the staircase as a metaphor to explain that we should have faith in our daily lives to complete our journey, even when we do not see the whole picture or know what the end results will be.

For a long time, my husband was accountable. I was getting comfortable in our marriage as far as regaining trust, then he begins to slip into darkness. One foot in the home, church and the other in the streets. One day, I got down on my knees to pray about the situation. I told God I felt like a hypocrite because I am serving Him, but my husband was straggling the fence (like God did not know). Then I asked God if I got a divorce a second time, would He forgive me? Could he still use me in ministry? I heard one word, "endure," I said in my spirit, *what does that mean Lord? Does that mean I must endure until I die?* And as clear as I am writing these words down, the Holy Spirit spoke to me and said, endure until the end of the situation. I got up off my knees both confused and annoyed at God. That was not the answer I was looking for and I did not want to endure another day! I was thinking about why a loving God would want His child, who is serving Him and His children to endure feelings of disrespect and hurt. But trust and believe, God always knows what is best for His children. Even when we do not understand. God sees the end as well as the beginning. Therefore, I continued my journey in faith that things would work out for our good. Things did not get better for a long while. The devil was trying to use my husband to get me off my assignment in ministry. But I continued serving in ministry and studying. My husband would tell me to continue my journey with the Lord and in ministry and he would say to me, allow God to do the work in him.

Now, the big turning point for him happened when the final incident with infidelity became a spiritual warfare.

Unfortunately, his brother got into an automobile accident, and after being discharged from the hospital, he was placed in a nursing facility for rehabilitation. My husband visited him during the weekdays. And I would pick up my mother-in-law after church on Sundays and we would visit him. It was this one CNA (certified nursing assistant) who took care of the brother, and I noticed that she was extremely attentive towards him, of which the family was grateful. She and my husband had become very friendly. In fact, they started having an affair. She was in my face smiling and being attentive towards my brother-in-law, calling him her boyfriend, all the while, my husband was her boyfriend. I began noticing some things; for example, a picture that I was in with my husband was missing off the brother's poster board. I also noticed that my husband never wanted to go visit with his brother when we were together. On one occasion, both his mother and I, along with my husband, had attended a funeral, and on the way home, she asked him to stop by the facility. He drove there, but upon arrival, he explained that his brother may be in therapy session and that we should remain in the car, and he would go up to check on him first. He comes back to the car and tells us that we could not come up. Again, I'm feeling a bit uncomfortable with his report – so I discern that something was strange or peculiar in my spirit; it was as if he did not want the nursing staff to know I was his wife – and behold, my intuition was correct.

One late night, I heard him talking on the phone downstairs and since I was awakened, I felt thirsty, so I got up to go get a drink of water. He was sitting on the sofa in the basement watching television. As I came down the stairs, I could hear talking, so I tiptoed down the steps and stood at the bottom of the stairs, and I listened to his conversation, but I could not hear what he was saying but I just knew it had to be a woman. Just like that, I found out he was involved with another woman. I walked into the room. When he looked up, I was standing there right behind him. He hung up the phone immediately. I told him that I had been standing there for a while, so don't even try to lie. I told him that I heard everything he said to her, that they plan on getting together the next day. The woman tried calling back and I tried to grab the phone out of his hand, but he held the phone away from me, hanging it up every time she called back.

He acknowledged that he still had a problem with infidelity, and he explained that he knew what he needed to do to prevent the behavior. He assured me that he did not want to separate or get a divorce. He promised he would take care of the situation and be accountable. During this time, I was studying to become a minister. We had already completed counseling; we had the resources and the tools –we just had to act on what we had learned.

The first thing he had to do was break off the relationship. He told me that he would speak to her in person and tell her he can't see her anymore. He asked me to allow him time to correct the situation. It was hard but I put my trust in the Lord to help us work things out. Shortly after that incident, I went out of town for a work conference in Florida. During our off time, my colleague (who is a Reverend) and I visited the Holy Land Experience. It was amazing! We took Holy Communion in the Upper Room, saw a play on the Resurrection of Christ, there was a replica of the Tabernacle of Moses, the Tree of Life, and on the Tree of Life, you could write prayers and nail them on the tree. I wrote a prayer of confession, repentance, and re-dedication to Christ. I wanted to make sure my heart was in the right place with God and the people in my life. I was able to spend some private, intimate time alone with God and listen to the Holy Spirit. The Holy Land Experience brought so much peace to me, and I thought to myself, that if this reproduction of the Holy Land was impactful then what would the actual experience be like! I hope to go there one day. I was on a spiritual high. Also, I wrote another prayer for my husband, asking for deliverance for him from the spirit of lust and any other strongholds the devil had on him. I asked God to help me forgive him and his mistress. I nailed those prayers on that tree, and I was confident that God would move in his heart.

My friend and I had dinner and we get back to the hotel late that evening. I was excited to call my husband and tell him about my amazing day. I called him on his cellular phone and asked if he was home so that we could talk. He said, yes, he was watching television. I began to share about my day's experiences, and I shared about my prayers that I nailed to the tree, but during our conversation, the phone kept going in and out, so I said, I can call you on the house-landline number, but he insisted that he could hear me fine. I continued talking but the phone went out once again, and he said *Hello! Hello!* But he could not hear me say hello back. Then I heard him say, "*Aww man...she is getting ready to call the house!*" and then he hung up the phone so when I heard him say that my heart dropped. I was so disappointed in him, and I did not call him back. I called my neighbor and asked if any cars were in our driveway. I had told the neighbor that I was out of town, and that I was calling home, but no one answered the phone, so the neighbor replied, it looks like no one is home. So, my husband had just lied to me, with the woman in his presence, I could hear the television, and him telling someone, that I was going to call the house phone. That phone call reminded me of the Parable of the Sower explained in Luke 8 –the part where the devil comes to take away the Word that was sown.

Luke 8:11-13 "Now the parable is this: The seed is the word of God. Those by the wayside are the ones who hear; then the devil comes and takes away the word out of their hearts, lest they should believe and be saved. But the ones on the rock are those who, when they hear, receive the word with joy; and these have no root, who believe for a while and in time of temptation fall away."

Just that quickly, after having amazing experiences earlier that day, hearing the Word, the devil comes to try and take away the seed sown, the joy, and the prayers for my marriage, even the faith in my prayers, and the Word of the Lord about the resurrection and love of Christ out of my heart. When my husband called back, I told him what I had heard and that I had contacted the neighbor. My husband was in his car by then, driving home, he said, that he apologized for lying. When he arrived home, he called from the house phone to prove to me that he was there. But how would I know if he didn't leave right back out of the house after the call? All trust was gone. He said he realized he must stop living the way he was living. I was so disappointed in him (yet again), but at this point, I felt there was nothing I could do for him, I prayed for him, I attempted to regain and exercise my trust in him, and as he suggested to me a few weeks earlier, I needed to focus on ministry so, I did because I could not keep allowing him to get me off my spiritual path. I was hurting but I had to intentionally not care about what he was doing anymore; I turned him completely this time over to the Lord. The Lord could take care of the situation better than me. I was allowing the devil to take away God's Word from my heart. The next day, I shared with my colleague about the night before. I had expected her to be surprised and feel some type of anger along with me. But she simply said, trust that God heard your prayer –the prayer you nailed on that tree. Trust the process and be at peace. She acted as if what had happened was nothing God could not handle. She said the devil was exposed, and that is all that happened. She reminded me to keep the faith and continue praying for my husband. In time, the manifestation of my prayers became a reality. My husband started changing, he returned to the man I married and fell in love with.

A year later, we went on a trip to New Orleans because my husband was attending a men's Christian conference. My sister-girlfriend lived there so I thought it would be a good time to visit her. While spending time with her, she shared how she keeps up with our other friends on Facebook and she showed me how to use Facebook. I started researching different people's names and looking at their pages. Of course, a bit curious, I put my husband's mistress's name in the search engine bar and when I saw her face, I said to myself, I know her from somewhere, as I looked through her pages, I saw her in scrubs and it hit me, she's the young African CNA from the nursing home my brother-in-law was in. I was about to fall out of my chair as I was setting on a barstool. I could not believe it. That woman was right under my nose, smiling in my face. I thought to myself, I would have known this a year ago if I had a Facebook account. That same night I could not sleep, and my sister-girlfriend was going to drop me off back at our hotel the next morning. But I could not wait until the next morning to speak with my husband. I was on the phone with him most of that night whispering to him about how embarrassed, humiliated, hurt, and angry I was to find out who she was. The next morning when I arrived at our hotel room, he was waiting for me. He sat me down and got on his knees right in front of my face and apologized, wiping the tears from my eyes. He said that he was sincerely sorry. Right then and there he placed his hand on the Bible and he swore that he would never hurt me with infidelity ever again. This was a whole year later after the infidelity incidents, but it hurt still, the more, as if I had just found out. Our marriage has been a model of how you can overcome all types of adversities. It was a wise choice he made to not get involved with infidelity from that point forward. And it was a wise choice for me to forgive him and continue to work on our marriage. We are now like Jenny and Forrest

Grump, "Peas, and Carrots". We simply go together. We are best friends and lovers, and we are now, truly one.

LESSON LEARNED:

Through all the trials and tribulations in life, having a spiritual foundation is the key factor in turning people and marriages around.

God is Holy and being around spirit-filled people, will convict the soul. They are going to comply with the Holy Spirit, eventually. Darkness will never, ever prevail over light. In times of trouble, pray. Hearing and obeying the voice of God has great rewards at the end of the situation. We don't always know how things are going to turn out. If we did, we would not need God and a willingness to work on our issues. Accountability: We all need someone, or God to be accountable to.

1 John 1:9 *"If we confess our sins, He is faithful and just to forgive us our sins and to cleanse us from all unrighteousness."*

After all, my husband is truly the man God had for me and through it all, we got the victory through Christ Jesus. Finally, my knight in shining armor! He learned to love me like Christ loved the church and gave Himself for it.

Ephesians 5:25-27 *"Husbands, love your wives, just as Christ also loved the church and gave Himself for her, that He might sanctify and cleanse her with the washing of water by the word, that He might present her to Himself a glorious church, not having spot or wrinkle or any such thing, but that she should be holy and without blemish."*

Truly, as Matthew 19:6 states, "what God has joined together" in us, absolutely nothing can put asunder (us under or separate). We are blessed, and if sharing our testimony of trials and tribulations, will encourage or help another couple who may be struggling in their marriage to have hope, our story is worth every shameful and embarring situation we endured. It is about Kingdom building when we help our brothers and sisters to be fruitful, prosperous, and successful in marriage, and in life. Writing this book has been such a blessing to me –just to see where God has brought me from concerning all my unwise choices, "situationships" and the consequences I sustained along the way.

Our marriage –no doubts –is indeed ordained by God.

The End.

CHAPTER 7

This chapter is written to share my personal experiences regarding "church hurt". And, to encourage the reader (who may have been hurt by the church) to forgive, and, also, to help Christian leaders and Pastors be more sensitive to the needs and feelings of their parishioners. First and foremost, let me remind you that the word "minister" represents every level of Clergy, and it means to serve God's people. I heard folk say, "do not talk negatively about the men or women of God" but please understand that every born-again believer is a man or woman of God, regardless of a title in the church or not. Therefore, let's not focus on the people who caused "church hurt" but rather on the situations which caused "church hurt" and how I overcame it.

Folks, sometimes church hurt can be more painful than relationships outside of the four walls of the church. Personally, I thought men and women of God were super-spiritual, kind, loving, and sensitive and that they would always exercise the fruits of the Spirit.

"But the fruit of the Spirit is love, joy, peace, longsuffering, kindness, goodness, faithfulness, 23 gentleness, self-control. Against such, there is no law." **Galatians 5:22-23**

I guess I was being naïve again! But the "fruits of the Spirit" undeniably, should be the character of the Clergy. My thoughts about most Christian leaders, and people who declared to know and love God –who study and teach the Word of God– would be a little more conscious of how they treat the people of God and that they would be biblically-sound minded. However, I experienced verbal abuse, abuse of power, disrespect, rude (mean-spirited people), jealousy, and ill-treatment from the church. This topic can no longer be swept under the table, and ignored because Jesus is coming back very soon, for the church, and as God's Word states, a church without spot or blemish. (See Ephesians 5:27 "that He might present her to Himself a glorious church, not having spot or wrinkle or any such thing, but that she should be holy and without blemish.")

Now I understand that Clergy (including myself) are not perfect people, we have flaws and insecurities just like anyone else. I understand living by the Word of God is a continual process for us all and no human being is picture-perfect. But Timothy teaches how we should conduct ourselves in church.

1 Timothy 3:15 *"I write so that you may know how you ought to* *conduct yourself in the house of God, which is the church of the living God, the pillar and ground of the truth."*

I thought I was in a safe place, being in the house of God. But no, I was caught off guard. I did not expect to be hurt in the way that I was. Honestly, I felt like the lyrics in Vickie Winans' song, "Long as I Got King Jesus". "I've been lied on, cheated, talked about, mistreated, I've been used, scorned, I've been up, down, almost to the ground". So yes -I needed Jesus, most assuredly!

I was told that I needed to be like the pastor! No sir, I need to be like Christ and the best version of myself. Also, I was told that I needed to honor the pastor and his wife! No sir and ma'am! I need to honor all humanity, as unto the Lord. This pastor would share this scripture with us (the parishioners) to make us understand that we needed to obey and honor him because he is our spiritual ruler.

Hebrews 13:17 *"Obey those who rule over you, and be submissive, for they watch out for your souls, as those who must give account. Let them do so with joy and not with grief, for that would be unprofitable for you."*

With all my heart, the Lord knows I tried to fulfill my obligations to my pastor, but seemly my efforts were never enough or good enough.

When I met this pastor, who hurt me, he was a humble

man of God. He appeared to have such a pure heart about winning souls to Jesus Christ and he seemed deeply connected to God, as he shared how he would spend hours in prayer and study of the Bible. It was refreshing to see someone who loved the Lord so much.

So, when I experienced church hurt from him, I was confronted with silent devastation. I am sure that many people have experienced church hurt but nonetheless, it damages your whole outlook on Christianity and the people of God. Whether intentionally or not, I never realized it until it happened to me that when a pastor hurts you, the emotional trauma reaches the depths of your soul. And although people are human and make mistakes in leading others, church hurt can cause a person to walk away from the church and even turn their back on God. But the Bible tells us not to forsake assembling ourselves together in church.

Hebrews 10:25 *"not forsaking the assembling of ourselves together, as is the manner of some, but exhorting one another, and so much the more as you see the Day approaching."*

Therefore, Clergy and church leaders, if you want people to come and fellowship together, you must be welcoming and exercise "the fruits of the Spirit". God holds Clergy and church leaders in higher esteem because they are His workmanship on the earth, God's representatives, and God's spokespersons. Also, please understand this, there is an expectation on my part regarding the character (godliness) and a standard of holiness one would hope Clergy and church leaders possess. Clergy and church leaders are held with a higher judgment to fulfill the great commission and great command of God.

The great commission: *Matthew 28:19-20 "Go therefore and make disciples of all the nations, baptizing them in the name of the Father and of the Son and of the Holy Spirit, 20 teaching them to observe all things that I have commanded you; and lo, I am with you always, even to the end of the age." Amen.*

The great commandment: *Matthew 22:36-39 "Teacher, which is the great commandment in the law?" 37 Jesus said to him, "'You shall love the Lord your God with all your heart, with all your soul, and with all your mind.' 38 This is the first and great commandment. 39 And the second is like it: 'You shall love your neighbor as yourself.'*

If these two foundational scriptures are not the heart of the church, Clergy, and church leaders (the church) is in trouble because Pastors have a big responsibility in equipping the saints. Therefore, they must have a heart for the mission of the church, and not themselves.

Ephesians 4:11-13 *"And He Himself gave some to be apostles, some prophets, some evangelists, and some pastors and teachers, 12 for the equipping of the saints for the work of ministry, for the edifying of the body of Christ, 13 till we all come to the unity of* *the faith and of the knowledge of the Son of God, to a perfect man, to the measure of the stature of the fullness of Christ;"*

When I joined the church, I always jumped right into the mix of the ministry. I have over thirty years of experience in some compacity of church service. In this one church, I joined, I began to engage in any way to support the vision of the pastor. I had a myriad of responsibilities. Although it was a small congregation, and the services were held at a school, the power of the Holy Spirit showed up every Sunday. The prayers and the praise and worship were so pure and genuine. We saw signs, wonders, miracles, and deliverances during those early years. It was amazing and I loved it. Serving God's people gave me a feeling of purpose and something exciting to look forward to in life. The pastor's wife was initially excited that I had joined the ministry, in fact, she said to me, that she had prayed about my family becoming members.

I felt welcomed, and I felt that there was a great need for me there in those early years of the ministry. The pastor and I connected concerning his vision to reach young people and ways to grow the ministry. I saw how beneficial the ministry was to young Christians because specifically, the ministry had helped my children regain their spiritual focus. They were in a good place, continuing to seek and grow in God. My husband and I appreciated that, and even though he did not join the ministry, he was always there to support us in any way he could help. Then the church obtained a building and began to grow.

I was entrusted by the pastor wherein I took the tithes and offerings home every Sunday and deposited the money at the bank on Monday mornings before I would go to work. I had my own set of keys to the church and the security codes. I sowed into the ministry financially. I would use my personal credit card to purchase whatever was needed to fulfill the mission and vision of the church – as well as personal items for the pastor; whatever he wanted, I would try to make it happen. One of my many responsibilities as the Superintendent of the children's ministry, my team and I put our hearts into growing a fun, exciting, safe, and spiritual environment for the children to come and get equipped in the Lord. And the children's ministry grew fast. We would often use our personal resources to fund activities for the children, pizza parties, and snacks on Sundays. We conducted summer camps, movie nights, game nights, and all sorts of fun activities. We even had a basketball room which really attracted the kids to come to the youth center. I was proud of the work we did. I also had obtained computers from my job and donated them to the church to help the children with their computer literacy skills and the laptops for the church. I am sharing some details so that you can understand how I was hurt when the pastor, and his wife, started being disrespectful and mean-spirited toward me.

Fast forward, I became a minister in training, I was given more responsibilities and opportunities to teach Bible Study, conduct new members' orientation and do small group activities with adults. With all these responsibilities I had, anytime I needed my husband, he would volunteer and lend me a helping hand with his services, wherever needed. He even engaged in our small group activities and supported me as I was growing in ministry. He even attended leadership training as a part of the church.

So, one Friday, after training, was completed. I was speaking to a female pastor from another church (she is a personal friend of the first lady of our church). I shared with her that I had placed her picture on my collage wall of ministry leaders that I admired; my pastor's wife was standing there with us. So, on the following Sunday, she (my pastor's wife –first lady) gently took me aside and stated that she needed to speak with me about something and that she would be calling me on the phone later. When she called, she shared that the other female pastor questioned my motives for putting her picture on my collage wall, and I responded to her that it was because I admired her ministry, just as I stated to her at the training. Then she (the first lady) asked me if her picture was on my collage wall? I responded that I did not have a picture of her, at that time to post. Then, immediately, she goes into this speech about setting boundaries with pastors. She expressed that the female pastor was uncomfortable with me putting her picture on my collage. I really thought it was a compliment, however, it seemed to be an insult to both, so, I guess they felt as if I wanted something from the pastor. I was really shocked that we were having this conversation because to me, it reflected signs of insecurities, and the reason I say insecurities is because I felt the female pastor (questioned my character and motives) and the first lady (questioned my allegiance to her). I was confused and offended that they both thought negatively about what was intended to be a compliment; nothing more or less. I was outdone because I felt the whole situation was silly and immature coming from whom I thought were classy women of God, so I stepped back for a time.

Be watchful! Women, be your sisters' keepers! We are to lift one another up, not tear each other down. Please do not allow your insecurities to hurt your sister. I suggest that you pray first and ask the Holy Spirit to reveal the truth about your sister (or brother) before you approach them with the wrong spirit.

After that incident, a few years later I would experience yet another disappointing encounter with the female pastor. It was at a women's conference the first lady was hosting. By this time, I had left the church, but on special occasions, I would come back to support and visit, and believe me, I had no hard feelings towards anyone there. I had made many great friends at the church; we were like a family. However, at the conference, the first lady, the female pastor, and the guest pastor (who was ministering) all walked into the sanctuary. And as they passed by me, I tapped the female pastor on her shoulder to say, Hello. She looked at me (directly in my face), turned her head, and kept on walking. Then, when the offering time comes and the usher directs us to walk around to give our offering, I attempted to speak to all three of the ladies standing there. The first lady turns around and started talking to the person behind her, the female pastor looked the other way, and the guest speaker was the only woman of God who hugged me and spoke. I was the person who introduced them to her in the first place. Anyway, on that following Monday, I was talking to my colleague, and she asked how was the women's conference? I shared with her what had transpired with these women of God. And she was as shocked as I was about their conduct, so she encouraged me to call the pastor to find out what was the problem. So, yes, I called the pastor's office, and she, picked up the phone (she stated that she normally would not do). So, I asked her if I had done anything to offend her because she did not speak to me at the conference? She said, no, I had not offended her, rather it was dark in the sanctuary, and she did not recognize who I was. WOW, so we are not speaking to people in the house of God because we do not recognize them. Really? Then she begins to share, how pastors get hurt when their ministers leave the church; mind you, she only had one side of the story. Then I understood why she was "feeling some type of standoffish toward me". Bottom line, because the pastor and his wife had a problem with me leaving the church, I guess she had a problem as well, although I had not done anything to offend her personally. Also, she obtained one side of the story. She did not know, that when I asked my pastor to continue to cover me, (as I start a women's ministry -and not a church mind you) he said "No." He said to me, "Find another covering."

LESSON LEARNED.

Pastors, please understand that how you treat people matters to them, but especially it matters to God! You, of all people, must know and show God's love to everyone.

1 John 4:7-8 *"Beloved, let us love one another, for love is of God; and everyone who loves is born of God and knows God. 8 He who does not love does not know God, for God is love."*

Moving on...

The immaturity gets worse. And oh my! The gossiping!

The pastor would share parishioners' personal and confidential businesses with us (church leaders) as well as his pastor friends and colleagues. This ought not be! We (church leaders) were required to let him know what was going on with the parishioners. One time, however, a parishioner told me that the pastor warned them about sharing their business with me –like I was the talebearer, when in fact, it was him, the pastor! I was too afraid that if something got back to him of what I had said, I would get "sit-down" from my duties. Anyways, I could just imagine that he also shared what was going on in my personal life, and the problems in my marriage that I shared with him, so most likely, if a person does that, it's across the board with everyone. Well, I guess he thought that because he was the pastor, he should get a pass.

It was getting to be a very bleak and dark situation at this church, and along with my personal issues, it became mentally draining. But I continued to serve and support the ministry. I kept a smile on my face; I kept it moving, and no one knew I was suffering in silence. I did understand, it was about and for the greater good –the Gospel. Like all the other negative experiences in my life. I learned going forward to value and treat people right. It got to a point that nothing I did or said was right in his sight. One time I was to introduce the guest speaker, I read his Bio, and then I said, "After the musical selection the next voice you will hear will be our guest speaker."

The pastor got upset with me because he wanted to say a few words after I introduced the speaker. I was not aware of that; he never told me he wanted to say something. He stated all I needed to do was read his bio! I felt like saying to him that I am not a mind reader. I thought, you said, introduce the guest speaker! Normally, if he wanted to say a few words, he would have advised me early on, beforehand. It just began to be one issue after another. One complaint after the other. It's funny how I was the best thing since sliced bread when I initially joined the ministry. But as the church grew, and other abled bodies would contribute, that's when the disrespectfulness began to accrue.

Also, I believe the breakdown with the pastor is when the parishioners started coming to me with their needs. A lot of times, the pastor was not aware of how I would go about taking care of their needs by assisting them in various ways, like giving them gas money, feeding them, and loaning them monies even before they asked the church, out of my own personal resources. When couples had marital problems, I would spend time assisting them, being open and transparent about things in my own marriage (if I thought it would help them). Appropriately, the pastor started having a problem with me being engaged too much with the parishioners.

One time, he said that I love getting attention from the

parishioners because they were hugging and greeting me during a church banquet. Other pastors and leaders were there at the banquet as well, and they were at special assigned tables, but my husband and I were with the parishioners, and they showed us so much, love. I was confused about that comment because I thought that being connected with the parishioners was what he envisioned for the church –to be "about people". So of course, I was saddened to hear him say such a thing, because, serving God's people was never about me, it was "only" about the love of Jesus and service.

How that pastor started treating me, reminded me of Saul and David in the book of 1 Samuel. Wherein Saul set David over the men of war, and he was accepted in the sight of all the people. When David returned with the victory of slaughtering the Philistines, the women came out of all cities of Israel, singing and dancing in the streets because the victory was won! And the women answered one another as they played, with tabrets, with joy, and with instruments of music and song: Saul has slain his thousands, but David his ten thousand! And Saul got very angry and jealous of David because of their singing of praises to David, it displeased Saul; and he said, "They have credited unto David ten thousand, and to me, they have credited but a thousand: and what can he have more but the kingdom?" And Saul side-eyed David from that day forward, to the point he wanted David dead. But

David honored Saul as King, as a father-in-law, and as a great leader and warrior. And honestly, the pastor made me feel like David hereto; I honored him, but he was mean-spirited towards me.

He also expressed that I was getting too familiar and comfortable with him and that this was bringing contention between us. Personally, in my opinion, I did not feel that I was getting too familiar with him; rather, he was getting too familiar with me, because he was the one who called me any time that he had something to discuss regarding ministry. He would call me on my secular job while I was working. I would stop what I was doing to support whatever it was he needed. I am embarrassed to say, I would drop whatever I was doing at home to support him. But my efforts were taken for granted. If he called me on my cell phone, and someone was in the car with me. I would let him know, but he would keep on talking about whatever it was he wanted. Out of respect for him I did not want to be rude, so I allowed it. But when I called him one Sunday evening about church business and his wife answered the phone, she says to me, *"Don't you have a husband you should be spending time with on a Sunday evening?"* The first lady, "prim and proper" (WOW! And your husband constantly blows up my phone!) So, when the pastor says, I was getting too familiar, I respectfully disagree.

(See **Matthew 5:38-39**) *"You have heard that it was said, 'An eye for an eye and a tooth for a tooth.' 39 But I tell you not to resist an evil person. But whoever slaps you on your right cheek, turn the other to him also."*

Well, we saw a real-life example of turning the cheek when we saw Will Smith slap Chris Rock, on national television, and Chris Rock made a joke out of it. He did not slap him back; he did not press assault charges against his brother, but rather he took the high road (Choose the noblest, ethical, or diplomatic course or method, especially after or in the face of negativity or ill-treatment.)

LESSON LEARNED:

Reader, take the high road. God will bless you in the end. When conflict happens in our lives, we must make a wise choice to take the high road.

Okay, so moving onward. God gave me the vision to plant a non-profit Christian Women's Ministry just before I retired. I shared my vision, with the pastor, who initially expressed excitement about it. He was willing to help me, as a part of his ministry and he started looking for venues where I could hold services in the area I had planned to relocate. I informed him two years, in advance, about this. However, as time got closer to going forward with the plan, the pastor informed me that he had not heard from

God about it, and of course, I understood seeking God's approval before moving forward, so I had no problem with that. However, when I asked if he would *cover me —you know, intercede in prayer, and provide information to help me get going.* His reply was *"No"* his reason was, that I did not honor him and his wife enough! I could not believe those words came out of his mouth and that really broke my heart. I served and honored them for about nine years, and it was devastating to me how he reacted, so, when I got to my car, I broke down and cried, I had to pull over to the side of the road to get myself together. And like that, our relationship was over.

So, I reached out to *another* pastor and asked him to cover me in prayer, and if he could support me by allowing me to use his church on Saturdays for my ministry (this was the family church I spoke about in Chapter 1). This pastor agreed. And things were going well for a few years (again, as far as I knew). I continued to sow financial seeds into that ministry as well as into that pastor's life. Then out of the blue, he emails me and said, he had not heard from me (which was not accurate) and he stated that he did not know what was going on with the women's ministry, and that I could no longer use the church. This was not "church hurt", but worth mentioning because pastors need to understand how they treat people matters to God. The seeds you sow will reap a harvest, therefore, I encourage you to choose wisely because Jesus is coming back for the church.

God has continued to provide for me with the women's ministry, when one door closed, God opened another door. God never disappoints, which is something my apostle tells me! God has provided a new location at no financial cost to the ministry. Man will fail you, but God never disappoints! The mission is still being accomplished, and the great commission and commandment are still going forward, praise be to God!

I now attend a very nice church, with pastors and church leaders, who seemed to make Jesus the primary focus of the ministry, and not specifically seek people who will honor them solely, but rather fulfill the great commission and commandment of Christ. No, the church is not perfect because I and many others are there, but I feel safe there as I choose to make an appropriate season for healing from "church hurt".

May God's grace and peace be unto the Church. Amen!

CHAPTER 8

"Jesus said to him, "I am the way, the truth, and the life. No one comes to the Father except through Me." **John 14:6**

First things first! We must confess that Jesus is Lord; Lord over our lives. We need salvation through faith in Jesus Christ because He is the way to Father God, and if you believe this scripture, you know there is no other way to your Heavenly Father, the Creator of all things. Choose Jesus! We have the promise of forgiveness when we repent of our sins, and with these actions, we have the power and the ability to forgive others.

1 John 1:9 *"If we confess our sins, He is faithful and just to forgive us our sins and to cleanse us from all unrighteousness"*

When I truly –honestly met Jesus in the pardoning of my sins, I felt like the Samaritan Woman at Jacob's well (see John 4). Jesus knew all about her –the men she had been with because He said, *"...for you have had five husbands, and the one whom you now have is not your husband;..."* Jesus knew she was looking for love in all the wrong places. But He did not judge her. Rather, He revealed Himself to her and it changed her life, forever, when He said this in **John 4:23-26** *"But the hour is coming, and now is, when the true worshipers will worship the Father in spirit and truth; for the Father is seeking such to worship Him. God is Spirit, and those who worship Him must worship in spirit and truth." The woman said to Him, "I know that Messiah is coming" (who is called Christ). "When He comes, He will tell us all things." Jesus said to her, "I who speak to you am He. "The woman said to Him, "I know that Messiah is coming" (who is called Christ). "When He comes, He will tell us all things." Jesus said to her, "I who speak to you am He."*

My life changed forever when I chose to open my heart and allow Jesus to live big inside of me, especially when I got filled with the Holy Spirit and the evidence of speaking in tongues.

I will never forget that special supernatural day my thirst for love and acceptance was filled. I was not in church at this time when I had another encounter with God. I was home cleaning the kids' bedrooms. I was sweeping toys from under the bed, so I was already on my knees. Bishop CL Long was on the radio, noonday prayer, and he began to pray. And the Holy Spirit told me to stop what I was doing and pray with him. He said, Repent! The Kingdom of God is at hand, and I began to repent of my sins. I desired to be filled with the baptism of the Holy Spirit, which is different from the Holy Spirit that all Christians receive with Salvation.

So, when I was praying at home, I kept saying Hallelujah, thank you Jesus for forgiving and saving me, repeatedly. I began to repent of my sins, the past, present, and future sins, asking God to forgive me and cleanse me from all unrighteousness, and I agreed with God to turn away from those sins. And the next thing I knew, I was speaking in an unknown tongue. It seemed like I prayed for hours because I did not want to stop. I desired to be in fellowship with God because God began to fill my thirst for love with His presence. And like the Samaritan woman at Jacob's well, Jesus' love, truth, redemption, and acceptance of all people truly set her free! Jesus accepts us, in the same manner, no matter what we have done in the past, the present, or the future; this is amazing grace.

God the Father desires that all of us have salvation through His son Jesus, the Christ and that our hearts be filled and flowing rivers of living water, which is His Holy presence. We will have an intimate relationship with Him. When we receive Him through His great grace and love (and not fear of damnation), the yearning for love through people is filled with living waters and we are never thirsty again.

During my journey through life, I made unwise choices

in relationships, because I was looking for love and acceptance from people. I expected people to love me like Christ loved the church. But a person must know God to truly know true love because God is love, He is true love. And without receiving that Agape (unconditional love of God) in our hearts, we struggle through life, and it is truly hard to truly forgive people without the love of God. Like making unwise choices, you must choose to make a wise choice to forgive others who have hurt or offended you; forgiveness is for you, it's not for them, it's for you. Forgiveness sets you free and, if you can't forgive others, how can you expect God to forgive your trespasses?

Matthew 6:15 *"But if you do not forgive men their trespasses, neither will your Father forgive your trespasses."*

I choose to forgive and love everyone, even those who do not love me back, e.g., the backstabbers, the naysayers, the negative and toxic people, because I could not love or live the Zoe life in Christ while still harboring unforgiveness in my heart. The Holy Spirit reminded me of the love of Christ when I discovered how much Jesus loves me, and it's not that I loved Him first, but rather He loved me first and He became an atonement for my sins when He willingly laid down His life for me and you on the cross.

John 15:13 *"Greater love has no one than this than to lay down one's life for his friends."*

Therefore, if Jesus laid down His life for us, surely, we can lay down unforgiveness towards our brothers and sisters in our hearts, and yes, we can make a wise choice to forgive!

1 *John 3:16 The Outworking of Love*

"By this we know love, because He laid down His life for us. And we also ought to lay down our lives for the brethren.

Harboring "unforgiveness" is not worth losing your relationship with God, and unforgiveness is sin, so here are four key principles to release you from the sin of unforgiveness:

(1) Acknowledge you have sinned before God. **Colossians 1:14** *"in whom we have redemption through His blood, the forgiveness of sins."*

(2) Repent (means to turn away from sin). **Acts 26:18** *"to open their eyes, in order to turn them from darkness to light, and from the power of Satan to God, that they may receive forgiveness of sins and an inheritance among those who are sanctified by faith in Me.'"*

(3) Accept God's forgiveness. **Ephesians 1:7** *"In Him we*

have redemption through His blood, the forgiveness of sins, according to the riches of His grace"

(4) Forgive others. **Mark 11:25** *"And whenever you stand praying, if you have anything against anyone, forgive him, that your Father in heaven may also forgive you your trespasses."*

LESSONS LEARNED:

Make a Choice to Forgive!

It may be extremely uncomfortable, initially, as well as painful to forgive because you may think that you are giving that person a pass who hurt or offended you. Once I understood that forgiveness helped me to move on with my life, and once I forgave that person, I felt the power of the Holy Spirit over the devil's strategy, which was trying to get me to hold on to unforgiveness. And you will know that you have forgiven that person when you come around them, as you won't feel uncomfortable anymore. You feel no negative feelings towards them because you begin to see them as God sees them and guess what? God loves them just as much as He loves you. Now, the relationship may be a little different because you may have to set boundaries, but the heart is pure and free when you forgive. And you can talk about situations or even write about negative experiences without hurt feelings because you have forgiven those who trespassed against you. People say "forgive and forget" but we do not forget all the good and wonderful experiences in life, if the bad experiences cause us to harbor unforgiveness. Your experiences may help someone as it is my hope in writing this book. For me, it was not about forgetting, but rather forgiving, and letting the bad feelings and thoughts go.

Dependence on God gave me the strength to forgive. But I had to change my mindset and attitude by fellowshipping with God in prayer, reading scriptures on forgiveness and love, and, asking God to give me the grace to forgive others. His Word states His grace is sufficient.

Sidebar: GRACE – "God's riches at Christ's Expense"

2 Corinthians 12:9 "And He said to me, "My grace is sufficient for you, for My strength is made perfect in weakness." Therefore, most gladly I will rather boast in my infirmities, that the power of Christ may rest upon me."

Wise choices were always there to make!

Know this last point — if you do not choose wisely — there are consequences to unwise choices!

Peace!

ABOUT THE AUTHOR

For over 30 years, Melanie A. Taylor has faithfully and enthusiastically served in countless ministries. She is the Founder and CEO of "The Church Without Walls" (TCWW) Ministries. TCWW is a non-denominational ministry that reaches humanity beyond the walls of the traditional church.

Melanie takes the good news of Jesus Christ from the "seats to the streets". She leads TCWW Ministries based on the Great Commission stated in Matthew 28:19-20, "Go therefore and make disciples of all the nations, baptizing them in the name of the Father and of the Son and of the Holy Spirit, teaching them to observe all things that I have commanded you; and lo, I am with you always, even to the end of the age."

Melanie's service and experience in ministry include being Chaplin for several high school women's basketball teams, a teacher in New Members' Orientation, and a Superintendent of Children's Church. She has trained teachers and taught in the children's ministry. In addition, she was a Pastoral Executive Assistant and Covenant Partner Leader.

Melanie has earned a master's degree in Davidic Praise and Worship Theology. She teaches The Restoration of the "Tabernacle of David" in this "Final Glory of the Church" to prepare for the Second Coming of Jesus Christ. (2 Samuel 6; Acts 15:16.)

Made in the USA
Middletown, DE
25 May 2023

30934884R10116